Clawing at the Corral

NIGHTMARE ARIZONA
PARANORMAL COZY MYSTERIES

BETH DOLGNER

Clawing at the Corral
Nightmare, Arizona Paranormal Cozy Mysteries, Book Six
© 2024 Beth Dolgner

All rights reserved. No portion of this book may be reproduced in any form without permission from the publisher, except as permitted by U.S. copyright law.

Print ISBN-13: 978-1-958587-18-8

Clawing at the Corral is a work of fiction. Names, characters, places, and incidents either are the products of the author's imagination or are used fictitiously. Any resemblance to actual persons, living or dead, businesses, companies, events, or locales is entirely coincidental.

Published by Redglare Press
Cover by Dark Mojo Designs
Print Formatting by The Madd Formatter

https://bethdolgner.com

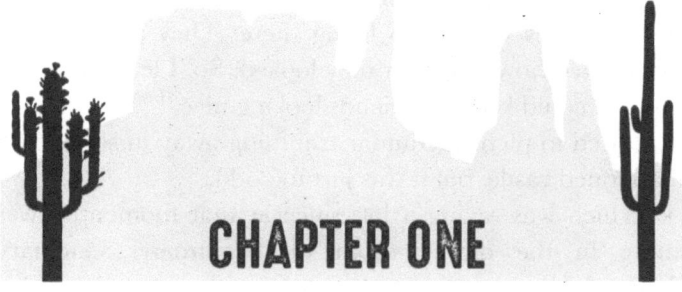

CHAPTER ONE

Gunnar's fingers curled around my chin, his claws gently brushing my cheeks. He tilted my head slightly as he gazed at me, his eyes dark against his stone-gray skin. "Look up at me," he said.

I complied, and Gunnar gave a nod of satisfaction. "I like this length on you, too. These split ends have got to go, though. I'm going to give you a trim, and I'll add some layers so your hair has a bit more volume."

"Sounds good to me," I said as Gunnar picked up a comb and began to run it through my auburn hair. I had kept my hair short when I lived in Nashville, but here in Nightmare, the longer look seemed to suit me better. It was more relaxed, like I was these days.

The scissors looked tiny in Gunnar's massive hands—or paws, or whatever that part of a gargoyle was supposed to be called—but I trusted him to do a good job. All three of the witches had raved about what a good hairstylist Gunnar was.

"How did you learn to do hair, anyway?" I asked as I watched bits of my own locks fall to the floor. The closest thing Gunnar had to hair was a green sheen all over his body that resembled a thin layer of moss. And it really was all over his body: Gunnar didn't bother with clothes. He looked like a living statue, albeit one with massive wings.

"I used to live in an old castle in Germany," Gunnar began. "It had been abandoned, and a few of us supernatural creatures wound up living there. They all had hair, and I hated how unkempt they looked. So, I learned to cut hair so I could keep my friends looking nice."

I tried to picture Gunnar trimming away in some dark abandoned castle, but it was just too odd.

Which was saying a lot, since at that moment, I was sitting in the dining room of Nightmare Sanctuary Haunted House, a gargoyle was cutting my hair, and a fairy was walking toward our spot in the corner.

"Hey, you two," Clara said in her childlike voice. Her violet eyes were bright with excitement. "We need to catch up since I've been off for a few days. Did you have a nice Thanksgiving, Olivia?"

I had been invited to join the Thanksgiving feast at the Sanctuary, but I had already made other plans. Mama and Benny Dalton, the owners of the motel where I lived, had practically insisted I join them for the holiday.

And, of course, they had also invited their nephew Damien Shackleford, because Mama took every possible chance to get me and my boss in the same room. She really wanted sparks to fly. Romantic sparks, that is. Not the magical kind I was pretty sure Damien would be able to produce if he unleashed his full supernatural potential.

"It was great," I told Clara honestly. "Mama and Benny are fantastic hosts, and I got to spend a lot of time with Lucy." Mama and Benny's granddaughter was only ten, but she was still one of my favorite people in Nightmare. She was the kind of kid who made everyone around her smile, thanks to her enthusiasm and unending energy. "But," I added, "Mama sent me home with so many leftovers that I'll be eating turkey until Christmas."

"That's nothing," Clara said. "I ate with my family before the feast here, so my mom insisted that I bring her homemade mugwort biscuits for everyone. And yes, they're as gross as they sound."

"I thought they were delicious," Gunnar said.

Clara made a gagging noise. Before she wandered off, she said, "The family meeting is in fifteen minutes."

"Plenty of time," Gunnar said confidently. In fact, he was finished with time to spare, and I had a chance to admire my trimmed hair in the bathroom mirror before I took my normal spot on one of the long benches in the dining room. I had thanked Gunnar profusely for offering to cut my hair, and even though he had refused to let me pay him, I made a mental note to get him some kind of thank-you gift.

By the time Justine Abbott stepped up to the podium to start that evening's family meeting, the rest of the Sanctuary staff had wandered in. We were missing a few people who had gone out of town for Thanksgiving, but it was a Sunday night, so we wouldn't be too crowded with guests, anyway.

Justine ran down the night's news and position assignments—I would be taking tickets at the front door, which was one of my usual posts—then her face lit up. "And, as most of you know, this is my favorite time of year! The Nightmare Christmas parade will be in three weeks, so I need all of you to be thinking about ideas for the theme of this year's float! And no, Theo, Have a Bloody Good Christmas is not going to happen."

Theo, who was sitting next to me, sighed dramatically. "She says no every year."

After the meeting, I was slowly making my way out of the dining room when I saw the three witches walking toward me. The oldest, Morgan, blinked up at me. Her white hair was so wispy it seemed to dance in the air around her wrinkled face. "We had a dream. About you."

"About love," added Madge, the beautiful witch who

3

looked like she was in her late twenties or early thirties. She tossed her long blond curls over her shoulder and looked at me sympathetically.

"But you weren't happy about it, oh, no." Maida looked to be about the same age as Lucy, but she spoke like someone far older. Her pointed black boots and short black dress made her look more witchy than the others.

"Be careful with your heart," Morgan warned me.

Before I could ask what they were talking about, the witches turned in unison and began to walk away. *Do they think I'm falling in love with Damien?* It was the only explanation I could come up with. He and I had been spending a lot of time together lately, and some of my other friends at the Sanctuary had been joking that there was something going on between the two of us.

That had to be it. I didn't bother to run after the witches to assure them I was definitely not falling in love. I hadn't even been divorced from Mark for a full year, so I wasn't ready to dive into a new relationship just yet.

As I made my way to the double front doors of the old hospital building that housed Nightmare Sanctuary Haunted House, I wondered just how many people were jumping to conclusions about Damien and me. Yes, we had been spending a lot of time together during the past month, but it wasn't at all romantic. We were both working on our magic. It had taken me a while to accept I was anything other than ordinary, but I was slowly making progress as a conjuror.

We still weren't sure what Damien was capable of. His mother, Lucille, had been an extraordinarily powerful psychic, but we still had no idea what kind of supernatural creature Damien's father was. Just as soon as we found Baxter, who had been missing since earlier in the year, we would ask him.

Because I had to believe we would find Baxter. Giving up simply wasn't an option.

There were always a few enthusiastic people lined up before the Sanctuary opened at eight o'clock in the evening. On this night, I propped open the double doors to see a group of what looked like college kids standing at the front of the line. I took their tickets and waved them on inside the entryway, where stanchions had been set up so visitors could wind back and forth between red velvet ropes before entering the haunt through a door at one side of the room.

Gunnar had run back upstairs, where many of the Sanctuary's employees lived, to put away his hair-cutting tools, and he was just coming down the grand staircase as the college kids made their way toward the haunt entrance. One of the girls let out a yelp, and another said, "Ooh, amazing costume!"

I caught Gunnar's eye, and we exchanged a smile. I had once said the same thing about him, before I knew supernatural creatures existed.

October had been incredibly busy, since so many people wanted to visit a haunted house attraction during the Halloween season. November had been slower but still much more steady than the number of visitors we'd had in the late summer. There were a lot fewer tourists in Nightmare during that time of year, when it was just too hot to be hanging out in a desert town.

Saturday night had been busy, and I had recognized a few locals who said they had family in town for Thanksgiving, and going to a haunted attraction was a fun, quirky way to spend time together. Now that it was Sunday, and a lot of people were probably on their way back to their own towns, it was much quieter.

At least until a large group came through, looking like they were going to a rodeo rather than a haunted house.

The six men were all wearing Western shirts with mother-of-pearl snaps down the front, and all but one of them was wearing cowboy boots.

"Hello there," one of the men, who was quite a bit older than the rest, said to me. I instinctively took half a step back because the man's gaze was so intense. "You're new here. We come every year on Thanksgiving weekend, and I've never seen you before."

"She's been in town a while," one of the other men said. He had brilliant blue eyes and sandy-blond hair that curled around the nape of his neck. His smile was bright in his tanned face. "Norman, you need to get out more often."

"Nah, I'm just fine hiding out at my ranch, thank you very much."

The man at the back of the group let out a loud whoop. "Let's go, boys. I want to get scared!"

The other five cheered, and as I tore their tickets and let them inside, they were loudly discussing which type of supernatural creature was the most frightening.

They were noisy, but at least they were having a good time.

I was tearing tickets for another group when a wave of cold washed over my shoulders. I turned to see the Sanctuary's two resident ghosts, Butch Tanner and Connor McCrory, standing behind me. Their ghostly forms shimmered in the dim lighting of the entryway.

"Shouldn't you be in your vignette, scaring guests?" I asked.

"Yes, we should," McCrory said, reaching up to tip his black cowboy hat to me. The former sheriff of Nightmare was always polite. "But we overheard some folks who went past us saying they'd spotted Billy the Bull Roper in the parking lot. We came to see if it was true."

"There he is," Tanner said, pointing toward the front

of the queue inside the entryway. A low whistle sounded from behind the red bandana Tanner wore over his mouth and nose. "I sure wish I could ride a horse as well as that guy."

"Which one are you talking about? And how do you know he can ride a horse well?" I waved a couple through even as I was turning to look at the rowdy cowboys, who were about to disappear through the door into the haunt.

"The one with the nice hair and the blue plaid shirt," McCrory specified.

Ah. The one who's apparently seen me around town.

"As for his skills," Tanner said, "Zach was once nice enough to take us to the Wild West Stunt Show out on the edge of Nightmare."

"At Norman O'Reilly's ranch," McCrory added.

"Did other people in the audience wonder why two ghosts were there?" I asked.

"Nah." Tanner waved dismissively. "We went to the matinee, and we're pretty invisible in bright daylight. We gave a few folks cold chills, but that's all."

The ghosts drifted away, since the person they had come to see had entered the haunt, and I knew they would be looking forward to trying to scare Billy the Bull Roper when he and his friends entered the vignette where Tanner and McCrory were stationed.

After work, I tried to drop into Damien's office to say hello, but the door was shut, and I could hear several voices inside. Since he was busy, I decided to head home. I had driven to work that night, rather than walking, since I had brought a plate of leftovers to snack on during my break, so I made my way toward the staff parking area.

I had to pass the visitor parking lot, which was really just a dirt field, to get to my car. The lot was nearly empty, but the six cowboys who had come through earlier in the night were standing in a group in front of several cars.

"I'd rather die than share the starring role with somebody!" I heard Billy shout.

The older man who had greeted me with such intensity leaned toward Billy. "We don't have a choice!"

Billy crossed his arms and glared at the man. "Well, don't blame me if he *accidentally* falls off his horse!"

CHAPTER TWO

I kept my eyes pointed in the direction of my car as I passed the men. They had stopped shouting, but I could hear low, angry muttering and grumbling.

Clearly, there was some kind of drama among the staff of the stunt show. I felt a wave of gratitude that the Sanctuary wasn't like that. The group where I worked felt like a family, and even though there had been a lot of drama when Damien had first arrived to run the haunt in the wake of Baxter's disappearance, things had been pretty calm lately.

I had just reached my car when I heard someone call my name, and I turned to see Maida walking toward me. She had wrapped a gray knit shawl around her skinny arms, but she still looked cold. Until I had moved to Arizona, I had no idea it got so cold at night in the desert, at least during the winter months.

"When can I see Lucy again?" Maida asked. "I haven't seen her since she was here in October."

I smiled. Maida and Lucy had hit it off the first time they met, and despite being from two very different worlds, they seemed to like each other. "I think the two of you should set up a play date. I'll talk to Lucy's parents about it."

"Thanks!"

Maida turned to go, but at the same time, I could hear the argument between the cowboys growing loud again.

"Wait," I said. When Maida looked at me, I held out a hand to her. "I'll walk you back to the front doors."

I kept a tight grip on Maida's hand as we hustled past the cowboys. Billy was yelling again about how he was the star of the show, and I caught something about "some upstart from the East Coast." I was worried a fight might break out, but the cowboys seemed content to stick to yelling for the time being.

Once I had seen Maida safely inside the Sanctuary, I had to pass the cowboys yet again. This time, they were moving toward their cars, and I figured the argument had run its course.

The drive home was a short one, since the Sanctuary was only about a mile from Cowboy's Corral Motor Lodge. My efficiency apartment was in the back right corner of the U-shaped layout, up on the second floor. It was small and looked like it hadn't been redecorated since the seventies, but I loved it.

Well, I didn't love the rust-orange shag carpet, but I loved the rest of the place. It wasn't fancy, but it was home.

The motel was my home because I had been broke when I arrived in Nightmare. And, of course, I hadn't so much arrived as I had broken down outside of town in my old clunker of a car. I should have known the thing wouldn't get me all the way from Nashville to San Diego, but starting a new life as far from my old one as I could get had seemed like a good idea at the time.

Mama had realized I was in a bit of a financial pickle —thanks to my ex-husband, Mark, who had driven us to bankruptcy before divorcing me—and she had offered to let me stay in the apartment in exchange for doing marketing work for the motel. It was a deal that worked well for both of us, and even though I was making enough money at the Sanctuary that I could probably afford a proper apartment somewhere, I didn't see any point in moving out.

When I woke up on Monday morning, it was that motel marketing work that I had on my mind. Mama had assured me things would get really busy around Christmas, so she and I had agreed to have a planning session over breakfast.

I stopped in the front office of the motel to say hello to Benny and to grab Mama. She patted her fluffy white hair. "It's a little windy outside this morning. Mind if we drive?"

"Whatever keeps your hair happy," I answered.

Mama drove a vintage red Mustang, so even though we weren't going far, it was still a fun drive over to The Lusty Lunch Counter.

Mama and I settled in at a booth inside the diner, which was designed to look retro. Our padded seats were upholstered in red, and there was a shiny stainless steel counter lined with stools near the kitchen.

As I looked around, I spotted none other than Billy the Bull Roper—*seriously, what kind of a silly name is that?*—sitting at another booth with a woman.

I jerked my head in Billy's direction. "Mama, tell me about the Wild West Stunt Show. That guy Billy and his friends were at the Sanctuary last night, and there was a lot of shouting going on."

Mama made a judgmental little "Humph!" She twisted around to glance at Billy, then leaned over the table toward me, keeping her voice low. "I've met Billy a few times. He's very charismatic, and it's easy to see why he's the star of the show. It's not just his talent on a horse. It's also his"— Mama held her hands up and splayed her fingers—"star power."

"And is he a drama queen in addition to a star? Last night, he was yelling about not wanting a co-star."

"I've never heard anything about Billy being a diva, but if Norman is bringing in a co-star, I can see how he might feel threatened. Billy has been leading that show for years, but the rumor is that the show's finances are an absolute mess. Apparently, they just about went out of business last year."

Leave it to Mama to have the town gossip.

"Maybe they're revamping the show to try to bring in more money," I mused. "I can see how Billy might not like having another leading man after being the star for so long, but I'm sure sharing the spotlight is better than being out of work."

"Tell that to a diva," Mama said with a wink.

After that, our conversation turned to the real reason we were together: marketing. It was what I had done in Nashville, but there, it had been high stress and long hours. Here in Nightmare, things moved at a much slower pace. Mama and I had a leisurely time of munching on bacon and eggs—and drinking plenty of coffee—while discussing things like the upcoming Christmas parade, which I had been hearing about since October. The whole town seemed excited about it, and Mama had an idea about recreating the neon sign that stood in front of the motel, complete with a giant yellow cowboy hat.

By the time we wrapped up our planning session and paid for our food, I had entirely forgotten about Billy and the stunt show drama. Billy had left with his companion at some point, and I had barely registered his exit.

But, when Mama and I walked out of the diner, I couldn't think about anything but Billy because he was standing directly in front of me, yelling into a cell phone.

"That's not what I was told!" Billy's face was beet red, and spit flew from his lips as he shouted. "You set up a meeting with this manager guy the second he gets to town. I want to see every line of that contract."

Billy ended the call and shoved the phone into the pocket of his faded blue jeans. With a growl, he turned and spotted me. "You're the woman who follows Reyes around, right? You tell him there's going to be another murder!"

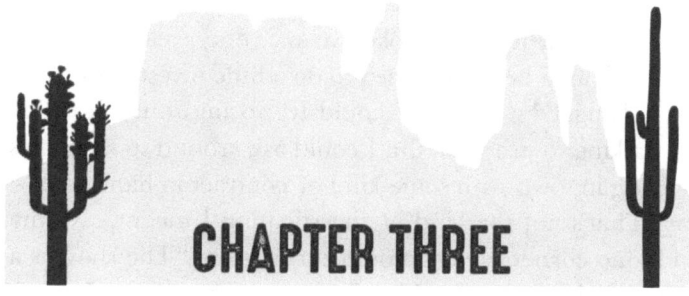

CHAPTER THREE

Billy stomped away from me before I could get a single noise out of my mouth. It was a good thing, too, since I had no idea how to respond to his threat.

I wanted to shout after him that I didn't follow Officer Reyes around. Billy made it sound like I was some kind of puppy trailing after Luis, but the truth was that I just so happened to stumble into murder cases. Or, sometimes, I stubbornly inserted myself into them. And, where there was murder, there was Officer Reyes.

At the moment, though, my relationship to Reyes didn't matter as much as the fact that Billy had just suggested he might be planning to murder someone. After the comment I'd overheard him make in the Sanctuary parking lot, when he had suggested someone might "accidentally" fall off their horse, this additional threat seemed especially sinister.

"Maybe I *should* tell Reyes," I said to Mama. It was as much a question as it was a statement.

"After what you said about Billy shouting up a storm at the Sanctuary, it sounds like he's a bit of a hothead." Mama gazed after Billy, frowning. "He's obviously good at shooting off his mouth, but that doesn't mean he's going to hurt anyone."

I nodded slowly. Mama was making sense. "Yeah. A real killer wouldn't confess before they even did the crime."

Mama turned and looked at me, one eyebrow raised. "Still, it might be a good idea to do a little investigating."

I shrugged. "I guess I could try to find out who Billy was talking to just now. Or, I could ask around to see who's arriving in town with some kind of contract in hand."

"That's not the kind of investigating I meant," Mama said, one corner of her mouth turning up. "The show is a little dated, maybe, but it's still a good time. If you haven't seen it, then you should."

"There's a daytime show, right? We could go today."

"I have to pick up Lucy at school. I can't go tomorrow, either. Benny has a dentist appointment in the afternoon, so I've got to mind the motel office, and then one of my oldest friends has a birthday dinner that night. You should get one of your work friends to go with you. I'm sure Damien hasn't seen the show since he was a kid."

Of course Mama was trying to get me to go to the stunt show with Damien. I had to hold in a chuckle at her not-so-subtle attempts to get the two of us together at every turn.

And yet, once we were back at the motel and I was in my apartment, the first thing I did was call Damien. I got his voicemail, so I hung up and figured I could ask him that night. I usually had Mondays off, but since we were still a bit short-handed due to people traveling for Thanksgiving, I had agreed to fill in.

I walked to the Sanctuary that night, partly because the weather was so nice. It was cool and clear, and the first stars were coming out as I took the narrow road that led to the old gallows. I was also walking because I wanted to clear my head. As much as I hated to admit it to myself, I couldn't stop thinking about Damien.

Not in a romantic way, exactly. I wasn't pining for him

or anything like that. Rather, after the strange warning about love I had received from the witches, I couldn't help feeling like everyone in Nightmare thought Damien and I had something between us.

Plus, there had been that one time when Damien's face had been awfully close to mine, and the way he had said my name right before we were interrupted had left me wondering ever since what he had been planning to say.

Zach was the first person I saw as I approached the gray stone building. He was standing outside the ticket window, which was under the portico where the double front doors were. "Hey, Zach," I called.

Zach ran a hand through his long rust-red hair as he answered with, "You're early tonight. Did you come to visit your boyfriend before work?"

I didn't dignify the question with an answer. Instead, I just shook my head and kept walking. Zach had been teasing me about Damien for weeks, and I worried that if he and Mama ever spent time together, they would have my second wedding planned in less than an hour.

Still, I had to admit Zach had been spot-on in his guess. I had arrived early to see Damien, but just so Zach wouldn't have anything else to tease me about, I waited until the door had closed behind me before I turned right and headed down the hall that led to Damien's office.

The office door was open, and I knocked on the doorframe as I entered. Damien had his laptop open on his expansive oak desk, and he was frowning at the screen.

"Hi," I said.

"Hey," he mumbled, not even looking up.

"I'm going to see the Wild West Stunt Show tomorrow afternoon. Would you care to go with me?"

There was a long pause, and I was about to ask the question again when Damien let out a long, "Umm…"

A few more seconds passed before he added, "No, I've got to get through these reports."

Damien hadn't looked up at me a single time, and I wasn't sure he had really heard my question. Whatever was on his screen was taking up all of his attention, so I turned and left without bothering to say anything else. I could have told him I had transformed into a Pegasus and flown to work that night, and Damien still wouldn't have given me the time of day.

I caught myself sneaking down the hallway, looking to see if Zach was anywhere nearby. His teasing was really starting to get to me, especially after the witches' cryptic warning about love. The coast was clear, though, so I quickly ducked into the next hallway, which led to the dining room and other staff-only areas of the Sanctuary.

Justine was just coming out of the costuming room, and she gave me a wave. "Hey, Olivia, you're early tonight."

I waited a beat, but she didn't add any commentary about Damien, so I just nodded and asked, "What are you doing tomorrow afternoon? I want to check out the stunt show."

"The rootin'-tootin', death-defying, heart-pounding Wild West Stunt Show starring Billy the Bull Roper? Count me in!"

I laughed at Justine's enthusiasm. "Are you a fan, then?"

Justine shrugged, her long chestnut waves swinging with the motion. "I haven't seen it in at least ten years. They used to have a TV commercial that described it that way, and honestly, it's just fun to say 'rootin'-tootin'.'"

In short order, Justine and I had laid our plans for the next afternoon. Her enthusiasm only increased my interest in seeing the show. I could tell myself all I wanted to that I was only going to see Billy in action and to get a feel for whether or not his threats were genuine, but the truth was, I wanted to see cowboys do cool stunts on horseback.

The next day, I picked Justine up at the Sanctuary, and she directed me to the edge of Nightmare. Really, I didn't need her help to find the stunt show, since there were faded wooden signs along the way to guide tourists to the right spot.

The parking lot was a dirt field, and to get to the small arena that housed the show, we had to walk past a red barn. There was a wooden fence attached to one end of the barn, creating a corral where a few horses were lazily watching tourists walk past. Beyond that were several small adobe buildings. Each building was labeled with a sign, like *Costume Department* and *Props*. Not too far away, I spotted a two-story white clapboard house that I assumed was where Norman lived, since he had referred to the place as his ranch.

Justine and I got great seats on the metal benches of the arena. We were sitting about halfway up but right in the middle so we could see all the action. Around us, tourists kept flowing in, and by the time the show started at two o'clock, the place was more than half full.

It made me wonder if Mama's gossip about the show nearly going out of business was incorrect. The ticket prices were affordable but not cheap, and there were hundreds of people there.

I was staring into the distance, mentally doing math, when Justine elbowed me. "It's starting!" she said enthusiastically.

Sure enough, three men had just ridden into the arena on horseback. They began acting out a scene, and between the cheesy dialogue and their outfits, it was clear they were supposed to be outlaws. One of them even had a red bandana over his mouth and nose, just like Butch Tanner.

Suddenly, there was the crack of a gun, and Billy came

riding into the arena. The audience clearly recognized him, and there was a round of applause as he guided his horse in a circle around the outlaws.

The show was a lot of fun, but there were a few parts that seemed a bit unrehearsed. After one particularly awkward exchange between two of the performers, Justine said in a low voice, "I don't remember some of this storytelling. And that guy in the fringed shirt is definitely new. He seems to be getting as much of the attention as Billy."

The conversation I had overheard in the parking lot of the Sanctuary came back to me in vivid detail. Billy had been yelling about sharing the bill with someone. Apparently, the man in the fringed Western shirt was that someone.

Despite the hiccups both Justine and I noticed, we applauded along with everyone else at the end of the show, as the performers came out and took their bows. When the man in the fringed shirt stepped forward and lifted his cowboy hat, the announcer boomed, "And introducing the fastest shot east of the Mississippi, Trent Nash, the Nashville Cowboy!"

"Hey, someone else from Nashville!" Justine said. "Do you know him?"

"Nashville's a bit bigger than Nightmare," I pointed out. "I've never heard of him, but he's a great stunt rider."

"Yeah, he's a nice addition to the show, even if it is strange not to see Billy getting all the attention."

Justine and I began to make our way toward the parking lot. When we reached the wooden fence surrounding the corral, I could see two of the horses sauntering toward us. I stopped and watched as they walked to the fence, and one of them pushed its nose in my direction.

"Hey, sweet horse," I said, stroking its brown and white face.

Justine pet the other horse. "I took riding lessons when

I was a kid. We should do some trail riding this winter. There's a ranch south of here that takes tourists through the hills on horseback."

"Oh, no," I said, shaking my head. "I would much rather watch other people ride them. I also took lessons as a kid. Well, I took one, and then I swore off horses forever. Being that high off the ground and at the mercy of a large animal was a little too scary for me."

"You say that now, but I'm going to try my best to get you on a horse."

"You might have to levitate me onto one to get your wish."

Justine looked thoughtful. "I've never tried moving a person before. I wonder..." Justine was telekinetic, and I'd seen her move small items, like beer mugs, using just the power of her mind.

I was about to assure Justine I was kidding about her telekinetically plopping me into a saddle when I heard a man call my name. "I thought that was you in the crowd!" the man continued. "Did you come here to see me?"

I had always assumed *it made my blood run cold* was just a phrase, but in that moment, it felt like I suddenly had ice in my veins. I knew that voice, and it was one I had never expected to hear in Nightmare.

It took every bit of willpower I had to turn around and look at the smiling man who was standing just a couple of feet away. His hazel eyes were shining with excitement.

"Mark?"

CHAPTER FOUR

Mark's smile faltered just a fraction. "Yes, of course. You did come here to see me, right?"

I shook my head. "I came here to see the show. I had no idea... So, you're... Do you work for the show?" *Keep it together, Liv!*

Mark laughed. "No. I've gone back to my old profession as a talent manager and promoter. I was always good at it, so I figured it was time to get back into the game."

I bit my lip so I wouldn't say anything I might regret later. It felt like a thousand emotions were surging through my brain, ranging from anger to complete bewilderment. With a sigh, I asked, "Mark, what are you doing in Nightmare?"

"I heard this is where you landed. Your brother told me. I figured if you're enjoying it here, then so will I." Mark was beaming at me again, and it gave off a distinct "used-car salesman" vibe.

Did he used to look at me like that when we were married? The way he was talking—and definitely the way he was looking at me—gave me a heavy feeling in the pit of my stomach. I worried Mark had followed me most of the way across the country because he was still broke, and he was hoping to lean on me.

"You're promoting the show," I guessed.

"No. Not yet, anyway. I'm managing Trent Nash, the new star of the show." Mark patted his short brown hair, then curled his fingers and inspected his nails. It was a strange, self-important habit he had picked up years ago, whenever he thought he had said something impressive. I thought of it as his own version of holding for applause.

"I was doing some digging to learn more about this town you wound up in," he continued, "and I found out the stunt show was looking for new talent. I knew Trent through some networking events, so I called him up, we pitched the show's manager, and here we are."

"How fortunate for Trent," I said. Beside me, I could feel Justine shifting uncomfortably. When I glanced at her out of the corner of my eye, she had a look on her face that clearly said, *What in the world is going on?*

I was kind of wondering the same thing myself.

"Trent arrived last Wednesday," Mark continued. "We thought he was going to have a week or two to rehearse, but they threw him right into it because he was so good. Today was his first show. I'm glad I got here in time to see his debut."

I felt a sliver of relief. "So, you came out here to check on Trent's progress. When are you heading back to Nashville?"

Mark patted my arm. "I thought I'd stick around for a while. After all, I just arrived yesterday!"

Oh, no. As the feeling of relief slipped away, it was replaced by a feeling of dread. When I had heard Billy on the phone, shouting about wanting to meet with a manager regarding a contract as soon as they arrived in town, I hadn't had any idea who he was talking about. Now, I was certain he had been referring to Mark. Billy must have felt like there was something fishy in Trent's contract with the show, and he wanted to confront the person responsible for making the deal: Mark.

Confront. Or murder. Given the other things Billy had said, I had to assume both were possible.

"Be careful with Billy," I warned. Sure, Mark was my ex-husband, but I didn't want him to become a murder victim. "He's not happy about sharing the spotlight, and I think some of his ire is directed at you."

Mark waved a hand flippantly. "Oh, he'll get over it. Hey, what are you doing tonight? I'll buy if you tell me a good place to get dinner around here."

"Oh. Um. Tonight? Well, actually—"

"You can't tonight, Olivia," Justine piped up. She gave Mark an apologetic smile. "Tuesday is girls' night. Sorry!"

"Speaking of which, we'd better get going," I said quickly. "I've got some work to do before I can go out and have fun tonight. Um, bye." I waved, turned, and walked as calmly as I could toward the parking lot.

Justine didn't say a word to me until we were in my car. "Was that who I think it was?"

I nodded and said *yes*, or I thought I did, at least. It was possible I just sat there and stared vacantly at the gas gauge.

"So that's your ex-husband." I felt Justine's hand slide over mine. "Are you okay?"

"Yes? No?" I laughed weakly. "I feel..."

"Overwhelmed?" Justine suggested.

"Yes." I paused, trying to find the right word for the way my heart was pounding and my brain was racing. "I also feel like I've been ambushed. I can't believe he decided to show up here. I left Nashville to get away from him and the ruins of my old life."

"Maybe we really should have a girls' night." Justine gave me a gentle smile. "I made that up since it sounded like you needed a reason to turn him down for dinner, but it might be good for you. We can drink wine and talk trash about Mark."

"Thanks, but Damien and I practice our supernatural abilities on Tuesday nights."

Justine's fingers twitched against my hand, and she made a snorting sound, like she was trying to hold back laughter.

"There is nothing going on between me and Damien!" I was trying to sound exasperated, but I was laughing too much for it to be effective. The laughter felt good, and I could feel myself calming down. I wasn't happy about Mark trying to insert himself into my life, but Justine and the rest of my friends at the Sanctuary would get me through it. I let out a deep breath. "I'm okay. Really. I just wasn't prepared to come face-to-face with him today."

"Or any day," Justine said. She let go of my hand and buckled her seatbelt as I started the car. "Exes shouldn't be allowed to show up unannounced like that. It's rude."

We spent the drive back to the Sanctuary talking about awkward encounters with exes, and I said goodbye to Justine, still feeling shocked and, honestly, a little horrified, but I also felt confident. I could deal with Mark.

When I was back in my apartment, I took a long, hot shower. The horses had kicked up a lot of dust during the stunt show, and I felt like a layer of it had clung to every inch of me. The shower also helped wash away the rest of my worry.

By the time I was dressed and had my makeup done, it was close to the time Damien picked me up on Tuesday evenings. Typically, we would drive out to the middle of nowhere so Damien could try to use his psychic abilities without accidentally flinging breakable objects with his mind. When his power had first begun to manifest, he went through a lot of dishes before he realized practicing at home wasn't the best idea.

I was ready to go a few minutes early, which would give me enough time to fill Mama in on Mark's arrival in

Nightmare. I could just picture the way her bright-blue eyes would widen in surprise. I texted Damien and asked him to pick me up at the motel office rather than at the foot of the stairs leading to my apartment, then made my way up to the two-story cinder block building that faced the street. There was a black BMW parked in front of the office, which meant Mama was probably busy checking in a new guest, but I knew that wouldn't take long. Soon enough, I would be able to pour out my story to her.

The motel office had a glass front door, and the bell over it tinkled as I walked in. The bell wasn't nearly as loud as Mama, though. "No, I will not tell you which one she lives in! I don't care who you say you are."

I sighed. "I'm right here, Mark," I called.

Mark whirled around and gestured toward Mama, who was standing behind the Formica counter with a thunderous expression. "She absolutely refused to tell me which of these rooms is yours. Why are you living at a motel, anyway?"

"Because I like it here," I answered.

Mark made a face that said he questioned my taste, but he wisely avoided saying anything more on the subject. "Anyway, I'm glad I was able to catch you before your girls' night. I'm brand-new in this town, Olivia, and I'll be counting on you to show me around and introduce me to the best places to go. Come on, grab dinner with me before you meet up with your girls."

Behind Mark, Mama mouthed, *What?* Out loud, she said, "Olivia, do I need to call Benny?"

"No." I sighed again. "Mama, this is Mark, my ex-husband. Mark, this is Mama Dalton. She and her husband, Benny, own the motel, and they've been very good friends to me."

"She wouldn't tell me which room is yours," Mark repeated.

"Because it's private information," I countered.

"Plus, I care about Olivia's safety," Mama added pointedly. "How was I to know you really are who you said you were?"

"Mark," I began. I didn't know what to say after that. Part of me wanted to tell him off, but another part of me suddenly felt sorry for him.

What's wrong with me?

And then it hit me. When I had shown up in Nightmare, I had been sad, angry, and broke. So, naturally, I assumed Mark wouldn't have followed me all the way to a tiny old mining town in Arizona if he wasn't in a similar state.

Be nice to him, I told myself firmly. "Mark, I'll be happy to give you some tips on good places to eat and fun things to do in Nightmare, but I'm not going out to dinner with you. You and Trent should be going out tonight, anyway, to celebrate his successful debut with the stunt show."

"I told him we'd go out after his show tonight. First, though, I thought you and I—" Mark cut off abruptly as the bell over the front door tinkled again, and someone stepped up to my side.

It was Damien.

"Everything okay here?" he asked, glancing between me, Mark, and Mama.

I opened my mouth to answer Damien, but Mark beat me to it. He plastered a bright smile onto his face and reached a hand toward Damien. "Hi, there. I'm Mark Phillips. I'm new in town, but I'm sure Olivia has mentioned me. She and I go way back."

There was a metallic *bang* to my left, and I turned to see the rack of tourist attraction brochures rock forward. Hundreds of brochures flew into the air and pummeled Mark as he raised his hands to ward them off.

CHAPTER FIVE

Mark had covered his head with his arms, and as the brochures floated down onto the shag carpet, he looked up wildly. "What was that?" His bravado was gone, replaced by confusion and fear.

None of us spoke for a few seconds, and it was Mama who eventually came to the rescue. "That must have been a big semi speeding past! Sometimes, I think the windows are going to rattle right out of their frames when they go by."

Of course, there had been no semi driving past when the brochure rack had tipped over. Mama and I both knew Damien had sent it flying with his mind. His power manifested when he was upset or angry, and clearly, meeting Mark had sent his emotions soaring. I had no doubt Damien knew exactly who Mark was and how he fit into my life.

Mark gingerly pressed a finger against his lower lip. "I think I have a paper cut."

He was lucky Damien had only thrown brochures at him. If the potted plants or some of the decor had hit Mark, he would have had a lot more to worry about than a paper cut.

Even as I was thinking that, I heard the bell above the door again. I turned just in time to see Damien leaving. He walked right to his silver Corvette without looking back, and in seconds, he was gone.

"Let's clean this up," I mumbled as I returned my attention to the mess in front of me. I began to pick up brochures, and Mama came out from behind the counter and set the rack upright again.

"I needed to reorganize it, anyway," she said with false cheeriness.

Mark stood and watched, dumbfounded, as Mama and I got everything neatened up. I thought about asking for his help, but I was feeling too stubborn to do that.

Finally, when the last brochure had been returned to its proper spot, Mark spoke again. "Who was that guy?"

"My nephew," Mama answered at the same time I said, "My boss."

Mark looked at me, his eyes narrowed. I recognized his jealous look. *Everyone else thinks Damien and I have something going on, so Mark may as well hop on the bandwagon, too.*

"He seemed a bit rude," Mark said quietly. "We don't treat people like that in Nashville."

"Damien is a gentleman," I said. At the moment, I was willing to overlook every jerk thing Damien had done since I had met him. For some reason, it made me bristle to hear Mark speaking negatively about him.

Mark's jaw clenched, then he gave himself a little shake and stood up straighter. "Come on, Liv, let's go out. I need to get out of here before another semi goes past."

"Oh! That's your BMW parked out front, isn't it? Where did you get the money for that?"

Mark ignored my question, and he seemed to realize I wasn't going to relent. "Fine," he mumbled. "I should probably be at the show tonight, anyway, to make sure it goes well. I'll see you later."

Mark breezed past me and walked out the front door. I

watched him go, then turned to Mama. "Now you know what Mark's pouty face looks like."

"What is he doing here in Nightmare?" Mama asked. "Did you ask him to come?"

I barked out a laugh. "Absolutely not! Him showing up here shocked me more than learning that supernatural creatures exist." I stepped forward and wrapped my arms around Mama. "I never thought he'd follow me here."

She gave me an affectionate squeeze and said, "Now, sit down and tell me everything."

We settled into two of the lobby chairs, and I poured out every detail, from going to the show with Justine to Mark hounding me to go to dinner with him. When I was finished, I said, "What kind of a vibe did you get from him?"

Mama pursed her lips as she thought. She wasn't a powerful psychic like her sister, Lucille, had been, but she was more perceptive than most people. "Drowning," she finally said. "He feels like someone who's trying to swim to shore in the middle of a hurricane."

"I guess he's a good swimmer, then. We had to declare bankruptcy because he spent every dime we had, and now he's driving a BMW?" I shook my head. "He's up to something."

"Yeah, trying to get you to go to dinner with him."

I stood up and took a deep breath. "You know, I always wondered how I would feel if I saw him again. Now I know. He was once right for me, but not anymore. As much as I disliked seeing him today, I'm glad to have this encounter out of the way. I feel better."

"You should be explaining all of this to Damien," Mama said.

I was a little scared of Damien at that moment, but I knew Mama was right. She wished me luck as I left the motel office and headed for my car. I was halfway across the motel parking lot before I stopped, turned around, and headed toward the street instead. I was going to walk to the Sanctuary, because I figured moving my body would help calm my mind.

The Sanctuary was closed on Tuesdays, and coming over the crest of the hill on the dirt road leading to it was always more dramatic when there weren't cars and people out front. The two-story building loomed up against the twilight sky, the weather-stained stone looking especially dark and ominous. There was an overgrown circular drive in front of the building, and in the middle of that was a sign that read *Nightmare Sanctuary Haunted House*.

The first time I had seen the former hospital, I had been going there for a job interview, and it had seemed so strange and scary. Now, as counterintuitive as it seemed, the old building felt comforting. My friends were inside.

The front doors were locked, so I knocked. About a minute later, Zach opened the door. He looked surprised to see me. "I thought you and the boss had practice tonight," he said as he stepped back to let me in.

"Something came up over at the motel." I didn't feel the need to hide the truth from Zach, but I also didn't want to dive into another retelling of my day at the moment.

"If you're looking for him, he's not here."

I took a few big steps backward and peered in the direction of the corner of the field next to the building, where staff parked. I could just barely make out Damien's Corvette in the last bit of daylight. "Yes, he is."

Zach stepped out and stood next to me. "Huh. Well, he didn't come in the front door. I've been in my office, and I would have heard him."

"I'll check out back, then. Thanks, Zach."

"He's in one of those moods, isn't he?" Zach was looking at me knowingly. "Whenever he goes outside, it means he's worried that if he stays inside, he'll break something with his mind."

I nodded. "I think Damien staying outside is safest for all of us right now."

"Good luck," Zach called after me as I turned and began to walk around the outside of the building. It was the same thing Mama had said, and I briefly wondered if I was foolish for trying to talk to Damien after what had happened at the motel.

I wasn't surprised when I rounded the back corner of the Sanctuary and found Damien sitting on top of one of the picnic tables out back, his feet up on the bench. His hands were clasped together tightly, and he was gazing up at the first stars of the evening.

"Hi," I said as I walked up.

Damien didn't answer. He didn't even look at me. His gray button-down shirt and black trousers showed off his muscular form nicely, and if I hadn't been so worried about talking to him, I would have stopped to appreciate the view.

"Justine and I went to the Wild West Stunt Show today. Some of the performers were here the other night, and one of them was saying some pretty threatening things. I wanted to learn more about them and the show, and I wanted to know if I should take my concerns to Officer Reyes."

Still, Damien didn't say a word, so I just kept on talking. "They've got a new star, a guy named Trent Nash. Imagine my shock when I found out Trent's manager is none other than my ex-husband. His being here isn't a coincidence. He followed me. I don't know why, and I don't know what he's up to, but it's not anything good."

Damien finally turned his head and looked at me. I had expected his green eyes would be glowing, which was a sign he was upset and his magic was building up from the heightened emotions. Instead, he just looked sad. "Why didn't you tell me?" he said softly.

"I was going to. Tonight, when you picked me up for practice." I climbed up onto the picnic table and sat next to Damien. "I asked you to pick me up at the office because I wanted to tell Mama about Mark being in town, too. Unfortunately, he got there before I did. I thought Mama was going to come unglued. He was being so disrespectful to her."

Damien's shoulder bumped against mine as he settled into a more relaxed position. "And I'm being disrespectful to you. I'm sorry. I'm not mad at you. It's just… I wasn't expecting…" Damien laughed self-consciously. "I guess I'm a little uptight when it comes to exes."

"You and me both," I said.

There was a nudge against my foot, and I looked down to see Felipe nuzzling my shoe. I reached down and stroked the chupacabra's snout, and he made a satisfied gurgling noise.

"I hope we're not interrupting." It was Mori, who was striding toward us gracefully. "I just woke up, and I thought I'd join Felipe out here."

"No, we were just chatting," I told Mori as she paused in front of me. Her golden eyes glanced between Damien and me, and she smiled just enough that the tips of her fangs showed.

Felipe hopped up onto the table and scrambled into Damien's lap. Damien seemed taken aback initially, but then he smiled and ran a hand along Felipe's grayish skin. "Who's a good boy?"

Just as quickly, Felipe lifted his nose into the air and sniffed. He yelped, then launched out of Damien's lap and took off toward a clump of scrubby bushes.

"I'd better make sure he doesn't eat anything he's not supposed to," Mori said. "You two have a nice evening."

Once Mori and Felipe had disappeared down a trail leading away from what I thought of as the Sanctuary's backyard, I said, "I don't like that Mark is here any more than you do. However, that stunt rider Billy has been making threats, and I know Mark is caught up in it, because he's the one who brought the new star of the show to town. Billy even told me there might be a murder."

"You think Mark is in danger?"

"I don't know. Mark might have thrown away all our money and asked me for a divorce, but that doesn't mean I want anything bad to happen to him."

To my surprise, Damien chuckled. "You probably have nothing to worry about. I've met Billy, and he's got a temper, but he's not a killer. All the recent murders have you expecting another one at every turn, but I think it's unlikely."

"You're probably right. Shall we go inside? It's cold tonight."

Damien and I walked silently from the backyard to his office, both lost in thought. Once we were in his office, Damien shut the door and turned to me with the same sad look he had given me earlier. "I really am sorry about giving you the cold shoulder, Olivia. And I'm sorry for my, uh, reaction at the motel. I showed up at the motel feeling good. I was looking forward to our practice session, but then when Mark introduced himself and I realized who he was, I suddenly felt this overwhelming—"

As Damien had been talking, his eyes had started to glow. At first, it was a soft light, but as he continued, the glow intensified, until I had to avert my own eyes from the brightness. I turned my head away just in time to see a blur of movement. Something was flying toward me, and I instinctively threw my hands up to protect myself.

CHAPTER SIX

I heard Damien shout "No!" even as the mysterious flying object collided with my shoulder. It was hard but not too heavy, and I heard it fall to the ground with a dull thud. I waited a few moments before lowering my arms, just in case Damien wasn't able to get his mind under control.

"I just did it again. I'm so sorry. Just talking about him made me—"

"Stop!" I reached toward Damien and curled one arm around his bicep. "Look at me."

I had prevented Zach from transforming into a werewolf twice, and I figured the same approach should work on Damien's power. Zach was always a wolf during the three days of the full moon, but if he got upset or angry at other times of the lunar cycle, he would temporarily change into his wolf form. Damien wouldn't transform into an animal, but when his emotions spiked, he was possibly more dangerous than Zach.

Damien's eyes were still glowing, and I had to squint a little as I looked at him. "If you keep talking about it, you're going to keep getting upset. Take a deep breath, and focus on me."

Damien gave the barest of nods, but he drew in a breath through his nose, then slowly let it out through his mouth. He did that a second time, then said, "Are you all right? I tried to slow its speed before it hit you."

"I'm fine. It didn't really hurt." I looked down and saw it had been a book Damien had subconsciously thrown. It had fallen open to a page with what looked like an old envelope inserted as a bookmark.

I bent down and picked up the book, snapping it shut so I could see the dark-green leather cover. "*Faulkner's Guide to Supernatural Creatures and Legendary Beasts,*" I read. Damien must have succeeded in slowing down the book's trajectory, because it was a hefty tome. If it had hit me at full speed, I would have been nursing a bruise on my shoulder. I told Damien as much, then added, "I guess this counts as practice."

"What was that inside the book?"

I opened the book again, and Damien plucked the bookmark out. It was an envelope addressed to Baxter, and the canceled stamp was dated June 21, 1973. "Who's it from?" I asked excitedly as Damien pulled a piece of paper out of the envelope.

"It's just a thank-you note for a donation to the Nightmare firefighters." Damien flipped the paper over, then shrugged. He put the note back into the envelope before returning the envelope to its spot in the book. "I know we didn't really practice, but I think we should call it a night."

"I disagree. Damien, we've been practicing together for weeks now, with almost no results. Your abilities manifest when your emotions are heightened, and most of the time, you're just in too good of a mood to work your magic. We should take advantage of your current emotional state."

Damien shook his head firmly. "I'm not going to risk hurting you again."

"We can go outside, like we usually do."

"The way I'm feeling, I might uproot a cactus and send it soaring through the air." Damien stared toward the fireplace, and I was glad to see his eyes had nearly returned to their normal state. "There must be a balance I can find. We've been focused on me getting upset enough that my power unleashes, but there has to be a way for me to use my power without the emotional aspect."

"You have to learn to control it," I agreed. "When you can control it, you can command it."

"Which means you—and even your ex—will be safe from me, but I'll still be able to explore my power."

"So, let's work on that tonight," I suggested.

"No. We'll try next time."

I knew from Damien's tone of voice that arguing would be pointless. He was right, though, that we had been approaching our practice the wrong way. We had been trying to get immediate results, which happened when he thought of upsetting things, like his fiancée dumping him. Instead, we should have been focusing on the control aspect so Damien could explore his power without having to go on an emotional rollercoaster first. It would be a slower path for him but a better one. It would be safer, too, as Damien had pointed out.

Damien apologized to me two more times before I left. I wasn't sure if he was still apologizing for his reaction to meeting Mark, for giving me the silent treatment when I had first arrived at the Sanctuary that night, or for having pelted me with a book.

Maybe it was for all of those things.

The temperature had dropped even more by the time I set out for the walk back to the motel, so I pulled my lightweight blue coat tight around me and stuffed my hands into my pockets. The cold was biting, but it was a distraction from the thoughts and feelings whirling around in my head.

When I got back to the motel, I saw Mama coming out the front door. She was locking up for the night.

"Hey," I called.

Mama turned and peered at me. "Damien is okay, then."

"Yeah. How did you know?"

"You feel better, which means Damien feels better." Mama waved her hand casually, like being able to read people's vibes, as she called them, and tap into the emotions of others was no big deal. She had once told me she began exhibiting signs of being a psychic when she was a preteen, but she had consciously tamped down the ability because she wanted to be normal. She had mostly succeeded but not entirely.

I filled Mama in on what Damien had said about needing to focus on controlling his emotions before we worked on his abilities, and she quickly agreed. "But," she added, "I don't think you've been going about things the wrong way so far, like you said. Damien needed to have these outbursts of power, I think, to prove to himself the importance of learning control."

"That makes me feel better. And now, I'm off to bed. What a day!"

"You're not kidding. By the way, a woman checked in about half an hour ago. She mentioned she's involved with the stunt show, too! How many new folks do you think they're bringing in?"

"No idea." I shrugged, then laughed. "I wonder whose ex *she* is!"

"Maybe you should introduce her to Mark, and they can commiserate together. Oh, I was going to ask you earlier, before things went haywire. Would you be able to pick Lucy up after school tomorrow? Her parents will both be working, and she's going to come here to get a little math tutoring from me, but I'll be wrapping up a doctor's appointment when school gets out."

I promised Mama I would love to pick up Lucy, then waved good night and headed back to my apartment.

"Haywire," I repeated to myself as I changed into my pajamas. It really had been a haywire day. Mark showing up, Damien's psychic powers causing chaos, and maybe, just maybe, Damien being jealous about Mark.

Is that even possible?

I finished changing, then went into the bathroom to wash my face and brush my hair. I took a moment to admire what a great job Gunnar had done with my haircut, then went to bed. As exhausted as I was, it took a long time for me to fall asleep. My brain kept going over scenes from the day again and again.

I finally fell asleep with the word *haywire* still in my head.

When the alarm clock next to the bed began to blare at eight thirty Wednesday morning, I reached over and slapped the snooze button without opening my eyes, then fell back to sleep. I did the same thing three more times. When I heard a loud noise again, I hit the snooze button even while realizing the sound wasn't my alarm clock, but someone at my door.

I rolled out of bed as the insistent knocking continued, instantly worried something was wrong. I hastily pulled my bathrobe around me and dashed to the door.

I didn't know who I had expected to find standing there, but it certainly wasn't Zach. He looked wound up but not worried, and I relaxed just a tiny bit. "Hey," I mumbled. "What's up?"

"Since your ex is involved in the stunt show, I thought you should know that Billy the Bull Roper was found dead in the corral this morning. He was murdered."

CHAPTER SEVEN

The last bit of sleepiness left me as Zach's words sank in. "Billy? But he was the one threatening to kill. How did someone wind up killing him instead?" I waved Zach inside, pointed to one of the chairs at the small round table, then turned on the coffee maker. This was going to be a lengthy conversation, I was sure, and I needed a hot cup of coffee to get me through it.

"Those are the same questions the police are asking, I imagine," Zach said as he slid into the chair. He looked around my little efficiency apartment. "It's a bit dated, but it's cozy."

"Someday, I'll ask Mama if I can replace the carpet. But, for now, let's focus on the important stuff. First, how did you find out Billy was murdered? And second, how in the world do you know about Mark being in town?"

"I have a friend who's with the Nightmare Police Department. He knows I do security for the Sanctuary, and he called this morning to tell me to watch out for coyotes. He said one, or maybe a couple of them, got into the corral at the stunt show last night and tore a guy up."

I pursed my lips. "Coyotes? But you just said Billy was murdered."

"I did. My friend went on to say the corral gate was locked up tight, and the gaps between the wooden slats of the fence are so narrow only small animals can get through them. The police don't know how the coyote could have gotten in, unless someone let it in. To make it even more strange, he said there isn't a scrap of evidence the coyote was ever there, other than the clawed-up body."

"What do you mean?"

"There aren't any paw prints, no bits of fur. Nothing. It's like the coyote covered its tracks."

"Billy could have been killed somewhere else, then his body was planted at the corral," I speculated.

"Maybe, but why?"

"Good question." I began to pace back and forth in front of my minuscule kitchen counter. "You know, this murder sounds awfully familiar."

Zach looked at me grimly. "That's why I wanted to be the first to tell you. I wanted to make sure you know I didn't kill anyone."

I stopped pacing and looked at Zach. "I know you better than that."

"You do now."

"But when I found Jared Barker's body all clawed up in front of the Sanctuary, it was natural for me to suspect you had done it with your werewolf claws." I paused, then added sheepishly, "Of course, I suspected you even before I knew you were supernatural. Sorry about that."

Zach puffed out his chest. "I'm kind of proud of it. I'm so mysterious that you thought I might have killed someone."

"It looked like Jared had been killed by an animal, but it was really Luke Dawes using a soil aerator from Jared's barn." I began to walk toward my closet. "Let me get dressed real quick, then we can go take a look around the corral. We need to look for something similar to what Luke used. Something that can simulate a coyote attack."

I stopped dead in my tracks as Zach began to laugh

heartily. "I'm sure your friend Reyes has already made the connection, Olivia. He'll do a thorough search of the property, and he'll be looking for the same kind of murder weapon."

"You're right." I sat down opposite Zach, feeling silly. Of course the police would be taking care of it. Billy's murder had nothing to do with me, so why should I get involved, anyway?

Even though it really wasn't any of my business, I couldn't help but start running through a list of suspects in my head. "Billy was threatening to murder someone," I said. "But who? He was also yelling into his phone about wanting to sit down and have a talk with someone, and based on the things Billy said, I think he was referring to Mark. Billy was also mad at the show's manager for adding Trent to the cast, and that means Trent would have had a target on his back, too."

"These are all people Billy might have wanted to kill, not the other way around," Zach pointed out.

"Yes, but maybe someone who felt threatened by Billy decided to act first. The show manager—I think Mark called him Norman?—might have killed Billy to get him out of the way and save his business. With Trent as the sole star, he could revamp the show and get out of financial hot water."

"That's a stretch," Zach pointed out. "Norman could just as easily have fired Billy."

"Okay, but what about Trent? Billy was really mad when he was here at the Sanctuary Sunday night, and after hearing him yell at Norman, I can just imagine him getting into it with Trent. Maybe the yelling turned into physical fighting, and Trent had to defend himself. Maybe this wasn't an intentional murder, but self-defense."

"Again," Zach said, "that seems unlikely. What did

Trent do, take the spurs off his boots and scratch Billy to death?"

I sat up straight. "Ooh, could spurs do that? Could someone have used them to make it look like an animal attack?"

Zach spread his hands, looking like he might start laughing at me again at any moment. "I don't know."

"But, as you said, Reyes and the other police officers will be looking for a murder weapon, just in case this was a faked animal attack like Jared's murder was." I sighed and leaned back. "If there are bloody spurs lying around, the police will find them."

The coffee maker chimed to inform me it was finished brewing, so I stood up and poured two cups of coffee. "Milk? Sugar?" I asked Zach.

"Yes to both, please. Light on the sugar."

As I grabbed the carton of milk from the fridge, I realized it had been a long time since I had fixed a cup of morning coffee for a man. Mark had always taken his coffee with two spoonfuls of sugar.

Mark. Could he have killed Billy? The Mark I had been married to wouldn't have raised a hand to anyone, let alone killed. But the Mark that had reappeared in my life so unexpectedly? Mama had said he felt like someone who was drowning, and I wanted to know where he had gotten the cash for that fancy new car. Mark had become increasingly reckless during the last few years of our marriage, even though I hadn't noticed at the time because I'd been so wrapped up in my career.

Plus, Mark had hidden our financial ruin from me until it was too late. He could be secretive, and I suddenly realized that, maybe, I didn't know the real Mark at all. Was he feeling desperate enough to kill Billy so his own client could have the entire stunt show spotlight to himself?

I shivered at the idea. As much as I didn't want to see Mark again, I also wanted to know he was innocent.

I finished stirring the milk and sugar into Zach's coffee, then returned to the table with both cups. "I know I should let the police do their work," I began.

"But?"

"But I don't think I'm going to feel comfortable until I know Mark is innocent. I don't need to solve the murder, but I need to know it wasn't him. This murder might not be any of my business, but I'm going to poke my nose into it, anyway."

CHAPTER EIGHT

Zach didn't seem at all surprised by my announcement. Instead, he shrugged affably. "Let me know how I can help."

I wrapped my fingers around my coffee cup, enjoying the warmth radiating from it. "For starters, you can help by answering my previous question. How did you know about Mark being in town?"

"Word travels fast." Zach gave me a wicked smile, but when I stared at him with one eyebrow raised, he added, "I think the guy did everything but put a notice in the paper. Apparently, he's been dropping your name every time he goes into a store or restaurant."

I wrinkled my nose. "Does he think being connected to me is going to get him somewhere?"

"It's a small town, and you're not exactly flying under the radar here. So, yes, I think he assumes any goodwill the people of Nightmare feel toward you will automatically be extended to him."

"Ugh."

Zach was smiling again. "I can't wait to meet him." I knew he was being sarcastic, so I didn't bother to respond. Instead, I just sipped my coffee judgmentally.

The rest of our conversation naturally turned to my old life in Nashville. Zach and I had talked about it before, of course, but this time, we talked more about what I had been like when I lived there. Stressed out was at the top of the list.

After Zach left, I immediately tried to call Mark. I thought I remembered his cell phone number, but when I punched it in on the loaner phone Damien had given me —it was actually Baxter's phone—I got an automated voice telling me the number was no longer in service. Either my memory was bad, or Mark had changed his number. Or, more likely, his phone had also been turned off when we were going through our bankruptcy proceedings.

My instinct was to rush right out to the stunt show so I could talk to Mark in person, but I was certain the police would still be crawling all over the place. Officer Reyes and I got along pretty well, but I knew he was tired of me popping up every time there was a dead body in Nightmare. I figured I would wait a couple of hours, when it was more likely the police would have concluded their investigation.

Waiting, as it turned out, was a lot harder than I had expected it to be. To kill the time, I walked to the front office to fill Mama in on the news. Of course, she had already heard it through the Nightmare grapevine.

After that, I took some laundry downstairs, to the communal washer and dryer that were in the back wing of the motel.

It was a long morning. Finally, when it was almost noon, I figured I could head out to the show without risking running into Reyes and seeing him give me that exasperated look he was so good at. It was an expression I was pretty sure he reserved just for me.

When I arrived at the stunt show, there were a handful of cars in the parking lot, including two Nightmare Police cruisers.

Great. The police aren't done, after all.

I considered turning around and going home, but I quickly dismissed that idea. I was feeling too impatient to talk to Mark. I knew I wouldn't feel settled until I'd had a chance to talk to him and could confirm he was absolutely, positively innocent of murder.

Yellow police tape was strung across one end of the corral, and I spotted someone in uniform taking photos while, nearby, another person was scribbling notes onto a legal pad. One of the officers had his back to me, and when he turned around, I smiled. I was trying to look polite, but I was pretty sure I looked sort of guilty. "Good morning, Officer Reyes."

Reyes sauntered toward me, not looking at all surprised to see me there. "I thought we were on a first-name basis now," he said. "After all, we do see each other an awful lot."

"Good morning, Luis," I corrected myself.

Reyes rolled his reddish-brown eyes, then gave me *that* look. "I knew you would show up. Your ex-husband has been talking my ear off all morning, so I figured it was only a matter of time before you arrived."

Zach had been right. Mark really was telling everyone he met in Nightmare that he and I used to be married. I decided to be totally honest with Reyes. "I'm here to make sure Mark isn't the killer."

"Do you really think the man you used to be married to might have committed murder?" Reyes looked like he didn't know whether to be shocked or amused.

"Not really. But it doesn't hurt to ask."

Reyes swept his arm in the direction of the arena. "You'll find him in the grandstands, along with everyone else we've been talking to this morning."

"Thanks. Oh, and before I go, there's something I should tell you about Billy." I filled Reyes in on the shouting match in the parking lot of the Sanctuary and the phone call I had overheard outside The Lusty Lunch Counter, followed by Billy's remark to me that I should inform Reyes there was going to be a murder. I ended with, "I didn't call and tell you that, because Mama and I figured he was just running his mouth."

"And instead of killing someone, Billy Curtis is the one who wound up dead." As I had been talking, Reyes had pulled out his small notebook, and he was writing furiously in it. "Interesting. Anything else?"

"No. That's it."

"Okay. Thank you, Olivia. This is good information." Reyes was still staring at his notebook, but as I began to turn away, he looked up and said, "Oh, just one more thing."

"Yes?"

"What did you ever see in him, anyway? He seems a little, I don't know, slimy."

I glanced in the direction of the arena. "Mark didn't used to be like this. He was always a bit of a hustler, trying to climb the ladder of success as fast as he could, but he didn't come off like an overbearing salesman back then."

Or, I thought, *maybe Mark has always been like this. Maybe he's not the one who has changed, but me.*

I was saved from having to wonder just how slimy I had been, myself, by a woman who walked up next to me just then. She was leading a brown and white horse by its tether.

"Are you sure we can take them back in?" she asked Reyes. She blinked her almond-shaped green eyes at him, which were red, like she had been crying. "They'll feel better once they're in their stalls in the barn again."

"Yes, the horses can be brought back." Reyes waved a hand between the woman, who looked like she might be in her mid- to late-thirties, and me. "Laura, this is Olivia. She works out at the haunted house. Olivia, Laura is the new horse trainer here at the stunt show. She has an incredible way with animals. She kept all the horses calm this morning, even with all the police sirens and people running around."

I wondered if the stress of wrangling horses under such circumstances was what had made Laura cry, or if she was grieving Billy's death. After a brief, polite exchange, Laura wandered off to take the horse back to its stall. I took that as my cue to leave, too.

When I got closer to the arena, I began to scan the people who were sitting on the front two rows of the grandstands. I recognized a couple of people as performers in the show.

I was looking for Mark, but I shouldn't have bothered. He practically sprinted over to me. "Olivia," he said loudly, "you have to help me! I didn't kill him!"

Several people in earshot looked over at us, and I tried to ignore the shocked stares. "Mark, keep your voice down," I said in an undertone. "Do you want to make yourself look guilty?"

Mark began to fiddle with the silver bolo tie he was wearing. It looked out of place against his oh-so-corporate blue button-down shirt, but I supposed he was trying to adopt a Western look to fit in with his new colleagues. "Sorry, sorry. It's just all kind of crazy, isn't it? Billy was the star of this show, and for him to turn up dead right after Trent and I got to town…"

"Do you have an alibi for last night?"

"No. I was in my hotel room." Mark turned his head away, frowning in the direction of the corral. "I can't believe this is happening. You got a second chance at a good life. Why can't I?"

I started to laugh. I couldn't help myself. Mark looked at me with a hurt expression, and I immediately explained that I wasn't laughing at him. Rather, I was laughing at how nearly identical our situations were. "When I showed up in Nightmare, I was broke," I said. "I took the first job I could find, which was at Nightmare Sanctuary Haunted House. On my very first day, I walked to work, only to find the body of a local rancher torn to pieces on the front lawn. It looked like an animal attack, too, but it was murder. You'll get through the ordeal just like I did."

"You found a dead body?" Mark said, horrified.

"Oh, that's not the least of my adventures in this town."

"Wow. We really do need to catch up."

I wasn't all that interested in catching up with Mark, but it was nice to hear him sounding like the Mark I had known. His fake smile was gone, and he wasn't being overly dramatic. He was just normal Mark.

"Officer Reyes doesn't really suspect you," I said in a reassuring tone. "We had a little chat about you when I first arrived."

"Good," Mark said. Then, in a barely audible voice, he added, "I can't afford a lawyer."

Mama's words came back to me. *He's drowning.* I remembered a friend in Nashville who had a BMW just like the one Mark was driving now. Mark had probably borrowed it because he couldn't afford to buy one himself. His car, his bragging, even his wide smile was all just an act.

"Honestly, the police don't seem certain this was a murder, anyway," Mark continued. "They say it's possible coyotes somehow got in the corral on their own, but they are considering that someone opened the gate to let them in."

"One of my co-workers said the same thing. A friend of his is with the Nightmare Police, so I got the scoop before I came out here today."

"While you're here, would you like to meet Trent? He's a really nice kid."

I agreed, since I was curious to meet someone who was on my list of suspects. As Mark led the way toward the adobe building with a sign out front that read *Costume Department*, I thought how strange it was that Mark had landed in such a similar position to mine. A new town, a new job, and a new dead body. Talk about déjà vu.

The costume "department" was really just one room, which was so stuffed with racks of costumes it was a wonder anyone could move around in there. In one corner, there was a three-way mirror with a small round platform in front of it. A man—not a kid, as Mark had called him, though he did look young—was standing on the platform. He had short dark hair that was slicked back from his forehead, and his gray eyes were wide and expressive. I recognized him from the show.

He's even more handsome up close. No wonder Norman wanted him to get top billing.

The costume designer was a woman who looked like she was in her fifties. Her graying blond hair was pulled back in a long braid, and she had three straight pins pinched between her thin lips. She was crouched down, tucking up one leg of Trent's pants. "Hold still," she admonished him. How she could talk without sending pins flying was beyond me. Years of experience, probably.

"Sorry, Darla," Trent said. He didn't sound sorry at all. He had caught sight of Mark and me in the mirror, and he craned his head around to smile at us. His smile, unlike Mark's, looked genuine. I could practically feel the charisma rolling off Trent. "Since Darla and I already talked to the police, we figured we'd get a little work done."

Darla gave Trent a look that clearly said the whole thing had been his idea.

"That shirt will need to be tailored a bit," Mark noted.

"If it's too loose, it's going to flap in the wind while you're riding."

"We're getting to that," Darla said as she stabbed a pin into Trent's pant leg.

Trent gestured at his red and blue plaid shirt, which had mother-of-pearl snaps down the front and gold fringe along the arms. "It's a great shirt, though, isn't it? I told Darla to give me the flashiest one she had. I figure the star of the show deserves to make a big splash in the grand finale!"

CHAPTER NINE

I gaped at Trent, who seemed blissfully unaware how crass he was coming off. His co-star at the stunt show—the man who was so upset about Trent jumping in to share the spotlight—had just been killed, and Trent was talking about himself being the star.

I had to wonder, too, if Trent's reference to a grand finale had been about the show's exciting ending or Billy's exit from this world. Even though I reminded myself I was only there to ensure Mark wasn't guilty, I was also aware that Trent was currently at the top of my suspect list.

"You're going to need something more," Mark said, waving a hand in the direction of Trent's legs. Compared to the shirt, Trent's faded blue jeans were just plain boring.

"Of course," Trent answered. "I'll be wearing my good-luck jeans with some leather chaps Darla has in the back room. They're vintage! Real, authentic Western wear."

"Neat," I said sarcastically.

"Although, this show's costumes aren't as high of quality as what we had at the show in Nashville," Trent continued.

I saw Darla glare up at him.

"You used to perform in Nashville?" I asked. "Why aren't you with the show there anymore?"

"Oh, we had some creative differences," Trent said lightly. "They wanted to take the show in a new direction, which involved bringing in can-can dancers and even a bit of singing. Who comes to a stunt show to watch a woman belt out cowboy songs?"

I had never been to the show in Nashville, and I could only nod my head vaguely as Trent described his experience there.

"We always had a packed house on the weekends, and I had a few locals who came out at least once a month to see me. They would give me the sweetest gifts, too. In fact, my—" Trent broke off as his cell phone began to ring. He was already holding it in his hand, and he answered with a loud, "Trent Nash here!"

Trent began carrying on a loud conversation, and he stepped off the platform and made his way to the door, presumably so he could have some privacy. Darla, still crouched on the floor, stared after him. If she could have spit the straight pins at him like darts, I think she would have.

Mark's phone rang just a few seconds later, and he wandered toward the door, as well. I caught the word "deal" as he went.

That left Darla and me, and we stared at each other with slightly widened eyes. "Trent is certainly, uh, confident," I said at last.

"He sure is. I'm not sure what's worse: a small-town, low-budget star at the end of his career, or a small-town, low-budget star who's still on his way up."

I tilted my head and peered at Darla as she slowly stood up and brushed off her gauzy black skirt at the knees. "Was Billy at the end of his career?" I asked.

Darla nodded. "Stunt riding isn't easy on the body. Billy was only in his forties, but he had collected quite a lot of broken bones and stitches over the years."

Only in his forties. I was forty-two, and I tried to imagine what it would feel like to get out of bed every morning after so many injuries. Billy had probably taken a lot of falls as he learned how to do all the wild stunts I had seen him perform on Tuesday.

"Was Billy as confident as Trent?" I asked.

Darla chuckled. "He used to be, back in his early days. He and I have worked this show for so many years that I didn't have a single gray hair when we first met." She touched a hand to her braid, then sobered. "I don't think it's sunk in yet."

There was no need for Darla to tell me what she was referring to. The entire cast and crew of the stunt show was probably in shock.

Other than Trent, I reminded myself.

I was about to ask Darla if she had observed any tension between Billy and Trent, but before I could get a word out of my mouth, Trent came back in. "Good news," he said jovially. "The moving company was calling with an update. I should have all of my stuff by the end of the week."

Trent hopped onto the platform, Darla stuck a few more pins into her mouth, and they got back to the fitting.

Darla was asking me how I liked working at the Sanctuary when Mark came back in and interrupted her. "Hey, Liv, why don't we go grab lunch? I'm starving."

"Oh, ah, well," I stammered. "I also work for Cowboy's Corral, so I've got to get a few things done before I go to the Sanctuary tonight."

Mark looked thoughtful. "Cowboy's Corral Motor Lodge. And we have cowboys and a corral here at the show. Hey, do you think they'd want to sponsor Trent? He could be the motel's official spokesman! Social media posts, local commercials, maybe an autograph signing at the motel..."

I put up a hand to stop Mark. "I think Mama and Benny have already allocated their advertising budget for December."

"What about for next year?"

I pressed my lips together impatiently. "I'll ask Mama." I probably wouldn't, but fibbing seemed like the only way to get myself out of the discussion. Or, maybe I would ask Mama, but I knew the answer would be no, because there was no way that wonderful woman was going to make a deal with my ex.

As I walked out of the costume building, I could hear Trent loudly declaring that he needed to add something "blingy" to his cowboy hat, too. I sure hoped Darla was a more patient person than me.

Laura was going past with two horses in tow as I reached the path between the arena and the parking lot, and I gave her a little nod. Her dark-brown hair was pulled up into a bun, which bobbed in time with her steps. "They're happy this is all over," she commented.

It's not over yet, I thought.

I was halfway to the parking lot when I heard Mark calling my name. I stopped in my tracks, closed my eyes briefly, and told myself to be kind. *He's trying to start a new life. Show the man some compassion.*

Even as I lectured myself, I was also steeling myself for him to ask me to lunch again. Instead, what he said when he caught up to me was, "You should talk to the previous trainer."

"Why?"

Mark ran a hand through his hair. "I've mentioned your name a few times around town, and word is that you solve murders. I figured you'd be looking for Billy's killer, too."

I nodded. He wasn't wrong.

"The old trainer here was a guy named, um, Leo?

Leon? Anyway, Billy got him fired. Maybe he let the coyotes in. He certainly knows his way around the corral."

"Do you know why Billy had him fired?"

"No. I can ask some folks here, if you want my help."

"I'm sure I'll be seeing you around. If you find out anything, please do pass it along to me."

Mark was smiling and humming to himself as he walked away. I didn't think he really wanted to help me solve Billy's murder. Instead, he wanted to help me prove him innocent. And, since that was the only reason I was even looking into the situation, that was fine by me.

The visit to the stunt show hadn't convinced me Mark was innocent, but my attention had definitely shifted to Trent. If anyone had reason to get Billy out of the way, it was him. Trent was clearly eager to be the only star of the show. Billy might have been approaching retirement, but I didn't get the idea Trent was a patient man.

I had lied to Mark about helping him get Trent on board as the Cowboy's Corral spokesman, but I hadn't been lying about needing to get some marketing work done. Once I got back to my apartment, I made a turkey sandwich with my dwindling Thanksgiving leftovers and munched on it while scrolling through the latest online reviews for the motel.

Only one review mentioned someone had recently been murdered in one of the rooms, and I figured that had been inevitable. The reviewer had given the motel five stars, anyway, so I wasn't too worried.

While I had the big, cumbersome laptop out, I did a quick internet search about the Wild West Stunt Show. I was hoping to find any references to the former horse trainer Mark had mentioned. I did find a couple of old articles from the online version of *The Nightmare Journal* which mentioned a Leo Whitehall, but they only referenced him as the show's trainer and choreographer. There was nothing about him getting fired.

Even learning Leo's name had been helpful, though, so I jotted it down on a scrap of paper and figured I could look into him more later.

First, though, it was time for me to go pick up Lucy at school. Nightmare Elementary School was a couple of miles away from the motel, and as I got close, I saw a long line of cars snaking out of the parking lot. I dutifully got in line, then shut off the engine, since there was still another ten minutes of school left. It was a cool day, so I only rolled the window halfway down. I leaned my head back against the headrest and closed my eyes.

There was a loud honk behind me, and I sat forward with a gasp. I had drifted off to sleep, and the cars ahead of me had moved forward. School was out. I gave myself a little shake, waved at the person behind me, then started the car and moved forward.

Lucy knew I was picking her up, and soon, I spotted her making a beeline for my car. Her curly brown hair bounced as she skipped up to the passenger-side door. Between her energy and her hot-pink T-shirt, she was like a ray of sunshine in human form.

"Hey, Miss Olivia!" Lucy enthused as she yanked open the door. She threw her backpack into the footwell, then scrambled in. "Thanks for picking me up!"

"You're welcome," I told her. I had worried she might be embarrassed to climb into my old car, which had faded paint and plenty of scratches, but she didn't seem to mind at all. Back in Nashville, when Mark and I had money at our disposal, I had driven a car much like the one he was driving at the moment. When I found out we were broke, I'd had to sell it and buy the only thing I could afford.

Lucy fastened her seatbelt, then we waited in the line to get out of the school parking lot. The whole time, Lucy chattered happily about her day at school. She told me what she'd learned in science about tigers, then listed off the states she had identified on the map during the social studies part of her day.

It wasn't until we were back on the two-lane road the motel was on that Lucy said casually, "Oh, and another thing. I talked to the dead girl today."

CHAPTER TEN

It had taken Lucy a while to realize the "mean-looking girl" she sometimes spotted on the playground was actually a ghost. I had figured it out long before she did, since she had told me the girl had a habit of disappearing in a flash. When Lucy realized she was seeing a ghost rather than a living girl, she had been curious rather than scared.

"What happened when you saw the ghost today?" I asked. I glanced at Lucy, who was gazing out the windshield thoughtfully.

"I did exactly what you told me to do. I said hello, and I told her I wanted to help her."

"I'm glad you took my advice. I think it's very likely she's haunting the playground because she needs help, or maybe she wants to pass along a message. Most ghosts don't hang out for the fun of it." At least, I didn't think they did. I really wasn't a ghost expert. The only two ghosts I knew were Tanner and McCrory, whose spirits were tethered to the six-shooters they had killed each other with in the middle of High Noon Boulevard.

And then there was Lucy's great-aunt Lucille, whose consciousness was still hanging around Nightmare. I didn't think she qualified as a ghost, though. By all accounts, Lucille had recognized how dangerous her psychic skills could be, so she chose to become a sort of roaming spirit rather than a person. Technically, that made her a ghost, but it was more like she chose to exist in a form that didn't involve a physical body.

With power like that, it was easy to see why Lucille had worried she might cause harm, and it was even easier to understand why Baxter had been so afraid his wife's abilities had been passed on to their son, Damien.

"What did the ghost do when you offered to help her?" I asked, returning to Lucy's own journey as a psychic medium.

"She disappeared." Lucy clucked her tongue. "So typical of her."

"Maybe she only has the energy to show up for a few seconds at a time. Still, I'm glad she was around long enough for you to talk to her."

"Yeah. I'll look for her again during recess tomorrow." Lucy said it in a matter-of-fact tone, and I wondered how she would react when, someday, she learned ghosts weren't the only supernatural beings roaming around Nightmare.

Knowing Lucy, she would be delighted, and she would insist on petting Zach's reddish-brown fur when he was a werewolf during the full moon.

"By the way," I said as I turned the car into the motel's entrance, "Maida said she'd love to see you again."

"She's so nice, even if she does dress kind of weird."

"If you like, I'll talk to your grandma about setting up a play date with Maida."

I pulled into my usual parking space at the back of the lot and looked over just in time to see Lucy's chin jut out. "I don't go on play dates anymore. I'm in the fifth grade now. But I would love to hang out with Maida."

I suppressed a snicker. "Okay, then I'll see if we can find a time for you two to hang out."

"I would like that." Lucy was already climbing out of the car, and she began to list off the things she and Maida would do. "We can go play in the storage room at the haunted house, and we can dress up in some of the old costumes. And later, we'll ask Mori if we can play with Felipe, and then we'll do our makeup like we're monsters, and..."

Lucy kept listing off her plans as I walked her up to the motel office. When she finally paused for a breath, I said, "And, Maida knows about the existence of ghosts. She'll be a friend you can talk to about the things you experience."

"That will be nice. I think my friends at school would make fun of me if I told them I saw ghosts."

I felt a stab of sympathy for Lucy. She was going to go through a lot of the same things the rest of her supernatural family members—Mama, Lucille, and Damien—had experienced, like learning who to open up to and how to live in both the normal and supernatural worlds.

Mama and I chatted for a bit before I went back to my apartment. It had been a big day, and I really needed some down time before I had to head to the Sanctuary for work that night. I lay in bed and tried to take a nap, but between Mark, Billy's murder, and Lucy's report of seeing the ghost girl again, my mind refused to quiet down. Instead, I stared at the popcorn ceiling for an hour before giving up.

The days had been getting shorter since my arrival in Nightmare back in August, and now that it was nearly December, it was almost completely dark by the time I reached the Sanctuary. The last bit of a spectacular pink sunset had already faded as I turned right at the gallows to follow the narrow dirt road that led to the building.

When I walked inside, I was nearly pounced on by Zach, who came running at me from the direction of his office. "It's the first night of the full moon, so I'm almost out of time. Did you learn anything?"

I began to tell Zach about my trip to the stunt show, and how Trent had seemed so unaffected by Billy's murder.

Halfway through describing Trent's behavior in the costuming department, Zach raised a hand to stop me.

"Sorry, it's starting," he said. I could even see the way his shoulders began to roll forward, which I knew indicated his body was beginning to shift into its wolf form. "I gotta go before I ruin another pair of jeans!"

Zach sprinted in the direction of his office, so he could undress before the transformation progressed any further. I had seen him shred an outfit before, and I imagined it could get expensive if he did that every month.

As I watched Zach disappear into his office, a voice spoke from just behind me. "I'm glad we get to see a happy Zach for three days."

I jumped, even as I realized it was Theo. He was the king of sneaking up on people. "You're up early," I remarked.

Theo nodded. "I always wake up early during the full moon. At least her arrival isn't as jarring for me as it is for Zach. I wonder what it's like to experience the wolf cycle every month?"

Gunnar had walked into the entryway as Theo was talking, and he paused in front of us. "I used to love watching werewolves run around during the full moon. Joyful and ferocious, all at the same time."

"Speaking of ferocious," Theo said under his breath, "what's with Damien?"

Damien was coming from the hallway that led to both his and Zach's offices, and even though he had his mirrored sunglasses on, I could tell he was glowering. And, if he was wearing his sunglasses, that meant he was afraid his eyes would start glowing, a sure sign he was upset.

"Which one of us is getting called to the principal's office?" Gunnar whispered.

"Me. I'm sure of it." I didn't bother to lower my voice. Instead, I stepped forward and met Damien halfway across the room. Without a word, I began to walk right past him so we could go into his office and talk.

I was surprised when I felt Damien's hand on my arm. "This way," he said softly. He was heading for the front door, and I followed curiously. If we were going outside, that meant Damien must be very upset. He was worried that if we went to his office, he might pelt me with another book.

There were already a few people at the ticket window, which was still closed. Zach would often open up early, but since he was busy turning into a werewolf, I knew Malcolm would be selling tickets for the next few days. Damien went past the people, turned left, and didn't stop walking until we had rounded the corner of the building. Since the parking lot was on the opposite side of the Sanctuary, we were about as secluded as we could be.

Once we were out of view, Damien stopped and turned to me. It was so dark on that side of the building I could barely see his features, and I wondered how he didn't trip and fall flat on his face with those sunglasses on. Only the light spilling out from some of the upstairs windows provided illumination.

"I assume you're already involved," Damien said tightly.

I opened my mouth to reply that, no, I was absolutely not romantically involved with Mark again, but I caught myself just in time. *Of course that's not what he means,* I told myself. Why had my brain gone there? "You mean with the murder case," I said.

"Obviously."

I gazed toward the scrubby bushes and low trees that marked the edge of the Sanctuary's property line. Stars were burning bright in the crisp night sky. "I'm looking into it," I said finally.

"Then you'll be interested to know I had a chat with Norman earlier."

"Norman? Oh, he's the manager of the stunt show, right?"

"Yes. Norman and my father were friends, so I thought it would be polite to call and offer my condolences. Norman seemed sad and shocked, as you'd expect, but there was something else, too. If I had to put a name to it, I'd say he sounded relieved.

My eyes shot back to Damien's face. Or what I could see of it, anyway. "Relieved that Billy is dead?"

"Relieved that Billy is no longer around, at any rate." Damien lowered his voice, even though we were alone. "He said something about revamping the show, and how losing Billy spares him some grief."

"It sounds like Norman was planning to get rid of Billy," I said. "Darla, the costume designer, told me Billy was coming to the end of his career. He was too beat up from years of doing stunts and falling off horses to last much longer. Maybe Norman wanted to fire him to make way for younger, more capable talent."

"Like the new guy, Trent. Norman went on and on about how much potential Trent has to be a big star."

"I guess the question is, just how desperate was Norman to get Billy out of the way? Would he kill to save his show?"

"You can ask him that tomorrow. I'm having lunch with Norman at The Silver Screen, and I told him I'd bring a marketing expert along with me to advise him on how to navigate this situation."

CHAPTER ELEVEN

My first reaction was to laugh, because Damien had finagled a way for me to get some time with Norman. Damien really hadn't needed to ask me if I was already involved with the murder case, because he knew me well enough by that point. Not only had he assumed I had already jumped headfirst into investigating Billy's murder, but he had also identified a suspect and arranged a lunch meeting with them.

At the same time, I was a bit dismayed at the idea of doing pro bono work for anything Mark was involved with. The idea of giving marketing advice to a potential murderer was disconcerting, too.

I tried to keep my tone light as I pointed out both of those things to Damien. Even in the near darkness, I could see the way his mouth set into a hard line as I spoke.

"I don't like you and Mark being in the same orbit, either," he said. He cleared his throat, then added, "I know it bothers you to see him."

"I wouldn't say it bothers me. I'm just not looking to spend time with the guy." *Is this why Damien is wearing his sunglasses? Is it the idea of me being around Mark that has him upset?*

I tried to push those thoughts away. Everyone making fun of me and Damien, plus the witches' warning about love, had me thinking about Damien in terms of romance and jealousy. I reminded myself firmly that there was nothing between us. He was my boss, and we were two people trying to figure out our supernatural abilities together. That was all.

At least, I was pretty sure that was all it was.

"I'll pick you up at twenty minutes before noon," Damien said.

"I can just meet you there," I said quickly, still thinking the very thoughts I was trying to get rid of.

"I have to pass close to the motel anyway. Plus, the restaurant has a small parking lot."

I agreed to let Damien pick me up, and as we both turned to head back to the front doors, I said, "Do you want to practice after work tonight?"

Damien nodded curtly. "Sure."

He was quiet after that, so I left him to his thoughts. Once we were inside again, Damien turned and headed down the hall toward his office, and I joined a few stragglers who were also on their way to that night's family meeting. Justine had already started addressing everyone by the time I entered the dining room, and I tried to be as quiet as Theo as I settled onto a bench at a nearby table.

I didn't appear to have missed much, anyway. As I turned my attention to her, Justine was saying there would be an electrician coming the next day to look at some lights that were on the fritz. When I felt gentle scratching against my right leg a few seconds later, I looked down and saw Felipe smiling up at me. Maybe smiling wasn't the right term. After all, I wasn't sure chupacabras were capable of making facial expressions like that, but the curve of his mouth and his little fangs gave the illusion of a smile.

I reached down and rubbed Felipe's ears as Justine moved on to that night's assignments. I was going to be in the lagoon vignette that night, alongside Theo, the siren Seraphina, and several others.

Zach joined me right as Justine was wrapping up, propping his huge front paws on the bench so his head and mine were at about the same height. His tongue lolled out, and he was definitely smiling. Zach really was happiest as a wolf, when he could get out of the ticket office and work inside the haunted house itself. He would run circles around the guests and howl, and they never suspected it was a real werewolf scaring them.

As I stood, Zach and Felipe bounded off together, heading for the door. They were probably going outside to run off some steam before we opened for the evening. The three witches walked up to me as I watched Zach and Felipe go, wishing I had the energy level of a werewolf.

"Such youthful exuberance," Morgan said. "I remember the days when I used to run free through the forest."

"How long ago was that?" I asked.

Morgan cackled. "Long before you were born, young lady!"

"Are you well?" Madge asked me. "You look rather out of sorts this evening."

"I thought all of Nightmare had heard the news that my ex-husband is in town. Somehow, you three must have missed the memo."

"Oh, we know," Madge said.

"We heard about the dead cowboy, too," Maida added.

"And so we want to know if you're well, dear," Morgan finished. "It's never easy when your past shows up to haunt you." Morgan looked significantly at Madge. A man she had once loved had unexpectedly come to town not that long before.

"You can relate," I told Madge. "It's strange, but I'm also okay, because I have all of you."

Madge reached out and squeezed my hand. "Yes, you do."

I thanked the witches for their concern, then made my way to the costume room to turn myself into a pirate. It wasn't nearly as dramatic as Zach's transformation into a werewolf, but I had developed a real fondness for my red coat with black lace cuffs. My matching red skirt and tall brown boots were nice and warm, which I was grateful for. I had gotten a bit of a chill while standing outside with Damien, but I knew that between my pirate costume and scaring guests, I would soon be nice and toasty.

Theo and I sometimes got competitive when it came to making people scream, and that night was no exception. It made the time fly past, and soon, the Sanctuary's last guests of the evening were gone, and it was time for practice with Damien. Except, when I got to his office, he was just coming out of it. "Fiona scared a guy so badly tonight that he fell over and broke some headstones," he said. "I need to go assess the damage."

"To the guy or the headstones?" I quipped.

Damien had taken his sunglasses off, and there was a hint of humor in his eyes as he said, "The only thing the guy hurt was his ego."

"We'll practice tomorrow, then." I was perfectly fine with that. My brain and my body were both hollering for bed.

That night, I got the sleep I had been so desperately seeking. I was tired from the day's events, and I'd had a lot of fun in the lagoon vignette, so I drifted off, feeling exhausted but content.

I woke up on Thursday morning looking forward to the lunch meeting with Norman. I figured it was worth giving up some of my time and knowledge about marketing if it meant I might learn something relating to Billy's death.

The Silver Screen was one of the nicer restaurants in town, which I only knew from talking to Mama. I had never been there myself. Still, it was only a lunch meeting, so I didn't want to dress too nice. I opted for a black skirt that fell just below my knees and a red and gray silk blouse. It was an outfit I had worn to many a dinner meeting when I lived in Nashville, and it was nice without being fancy. I was wearing low black heels, too, and I realized it was the first time I had worn them since arriving in Nightmare.

Damien was right on time picking me up, so when I opened my door at twenty minutes before noon, his silver Corvette was just rolling to a stop at the foot of my stairs. I slid into the passenger seat carefully, trying not to wrinkle my outfit.

"You look nice," Damien said appreciatively.

"Thanks. So do you." Of course, Damien always looked nice, especially since he was partial to three-piece suits. He was slightly more casual for our lunch meeting, wearing black trousers and a black button-down shirt. I nearly commented that he looked like he was going to a funeral, but the outfit worked with his lightly tanned skin and wavy light-brown hair.

"Tell me about Norman," I said as Damien pulled out of the motel parking lot.

"He's around my dad's age. That is, the age everyone thinks my dad is." Baxter was very, very old, though none of us knew exactly how long he'd been around. His long life was a clue to what kind of supernatural creature he was, but we needed a lot more clues before we would arrive at an answer.

"That means Norman is in his sixties or early seventies," I guessed.

"Yeah. He's been running the stunt show since I can remember. Billy became the star of the show twenty years ago, or somewhere around then. From what I remember, Billy made a big splash in those first years. Nightmare's tourism increased because people from all over wanted to come and see him. The show hasn't been as wildly popular in recent years, but it still draws a lot of tourists."

I held up a hand as Damien turned onto a road leading east. "You're telling me about the show, but I want to know about the man."

Damien gave a short laugh. "They're kind of one and the same. The show is Norman's whole life. He lives out there at the stunt show arena, every penny he has goes into the show, and rumor has it his wife divorced him because she got tired of competing with a bunch of horses and stunt riders."

"Wow."

"Yeah. Norman views Trent Nash as his ticket to retirement. He hopes a new star and an updated show will attract tourists in droves, so he can go out with a bang."

"People like that never really retire, do they? He's probably the type who will drop dead on the job one day."

"If that happens, let's hope it's not murder."

Damien had been right about the restaurant having a small parking lot. It wasn't noon yet, but there were only a few spaces left. The restaurant itself appeared to be a former movie theater, complete with a marquis above the front doors. It was in an area of town I'd heard referred to as New Downtown. After the big copper mine had gone bust, Nightmare had nearly become a ghost town. When it started to revive, High Noon Boulevard became a focal point for tourists, so a lot of businesses moved a few miles down the road to what had developed into a nice area of shops and restaurants. Like the old theater, a lot of the buildings in New Downtown looked like they were from the nineteen fifties and sixties.

Inside, the theater had been transformed into a beautiful restaurant, with lush red carpet, flocked wallpaper on the walls, and overstuffed leather chairs at every table. The movie screen was still in place, and a silent black-and-white film was playing. Tinny piano music played quietly from speakers.

"What a great place!" I enthused as soon as we were inside.

Damien didn't seem to have heard me. He was already heading for a table a short distance away. A stout, red-faced man with a head of thick white hair and intense hazel eyes stood up and extended his hand, and I recognized him from his visit to the Sanctuary.

When I drifted up beside Damien, he gestured to me. "And this is Olivia Kendrick. She's been a marketing professional for a long time."

"Norman O'Reilly," the man said, taking my hand in a firm grip. "I've seen you before! Sit, sit. I already ordered the shrimp cocktail for us."

No sooner had Damien and I sat down than I spotted Mark walking toward us. At the same time, the water glasses on the table began to vibrate. Some water sloshed over the rim of mine and onto the white tablecloth. Damien was not happy about our unexpected lunch companion.

Instinctively, I moved my hand under the table and found Damien's. I curled my fingers around his and thought, *Damien is calm. Damien is calm. Damien is calm.*

The water glasses stopped vibrating. Norman hadn't seemed to notice, and he was happily chattering to Damien, who gave me a brief glance out of the corner of his eye. There was a hint of a smile on his lips, and I knew he realized I had just conjured his calm demeanor.

Mark had a confident look on his face, which faltered just a bit as Damien turned to him and said hello. When nothing flew at Mark, though, he seemed to relax, and he sat down.

"I thought Mark ought to be part of our discussion today, too," Norman said jovially. "This boy has some great ideas."

A server arrived to take our drink orders and to drop off the shrimp cocktail. Once he had left, Norman leaned across the table toward me. "Now, tell me, Ms. Marketing Expert, how are we going to convince the people of Nightmare that I'm not a murderer?"

CHAPTER TWELVE

"Mr. O'Reilly," I began, but Norman waved a hand and winked at me.

"Just call me Norman. I don't know how you did things back in Nashville, but this is Nightmare, and we're pretty casual."

"Norman, then," I continued. "I'll be honest with you. I've helped clients put together company statements about death but never murder. This is new territory for me, but I'll give as much helpful advice as I can."

"I would sure appreciate it. I know we have to say something to the community, but I don't even know where to start. No one has ever been murdered on my property before."

"Then," I said carefully, "I suppose the animal attack angle has been ruled out?"

"Not at all." Norman looked around the table at the rest of us, his expression dramatic. "The police still think it might have been coyotes, but who let them through the locked corral gate? To make it even more bizarre, there's no sign the horses were spooked inside their stalls. If even one coyote had gotten inside the corral, they would have been so close to the barn that the horses would have smelled or heard them and panicked."

Again, I thought back to Jared Barker's murder. It was

looking a lot more likely that a human being had done the damage to Billy, even though they had tried to make it look like he'd been clawed by an animal. "How do you know the horses stayed calm?" I asked. "Are there security cameras on the stalls?"

Norman chuckled at that idea. "No, Laura told me. She's our new trainer, and she really understands those horses. She said there were no signs they were stressed."

If Laura was that instinctive about the horses, I realized, then maybe she could give me some more insight into what kind of scenarios might have played out the night Billy died. Norman thought I was meeting him to provide help, not to track down a murderer, so I said casually, "I'd love to talk to her. What a fascinating job she has."

"Not today, I'm afraid," Norman said, shaking his head. "The horses might have been fine that night, but all the police sirens and lights and people running around the next morning really did a number on them. Laura had her hands full keeping them calm yesterday, especially when she had to move all of them out of their stalls so the police could search inside the barn, in case there was any evidence there. She took the day off today to recover from the strain."

"I'm sure it was a difficult day for her," I said. "What happened to the horse trainer who had the job before her?"

Mark and Damien had both been watching my conversation with Norman silently, and as soon as I asked that question, I saw Mark's face light up. I was taking his advice to look into the show's former trainer, and he was delighted by that.

"Oh, Leo's pretty much retired now," Norman said. "He's as old as the rest of us."

Even as Norman was speaking, all four of our water glasses began to vibrate again. I focused on calming

Damien down as I once again took his hand under the table. I kept my eyes on Norman, but in my peripheral vision, I could tell Damien was glaring at Mark.

"I hope he's enjoying his retirement," I said, trying my best to both conjure and carry on a conversation. It wasn't easy. I rubbed my thumb over the back of Damien's hand, and the glasses slowly came to a standstill. I kept my hand in his, though, just in case.

"Billy should have retired, too," Norman continued. He looked sad, but like Damien had mentioned before, there was something like relief in Norman's voice. "He had earned a rest. I didn't tell him Trent was going to be his co-star until Sunday night. Even during rehearsals last week, I had Trent work on his parts when Billy wasn't there, because I knew Billy wouldn't take the news well. No star wants to be told they're not able to carry a show on their own anymore. Thank goodness we already have Trent, so the show won't need to close while we look for a new star."

Mark was beaming again, but this time, it was at Norman. "Billy's death is unfortunate, for sure, but I'm glad we're able to make this difficult time a little easier for you."

Yuck. Mark's comment came off as tacky, but neither he nor Norman seemed to realize it.

We talked more about Billy as we ate our lunch, but mostly, I coached Norman about how to address the murder, the kinds of words and phrases to use, and what sort of statements to avoid. Since I still thought Norman might have killed Billy, I couldn't help but feel a bit gross about the whole thing. Was I helping a murderer cover his tracks?

Finally, Norman seemed satisfied that he was equipped to deal with both the public and the local reporters, and as our plates were cleared, he moved on to talking about how great of an addition Trent had been to the show. Mark was enthusiastic about the subject, and Damien and I patiently listened to them go on at length about Trent's star power.

We all left the restaurant together, and once we were outside, Norman said a quick goodbye. "Sorry to run, but we've got the matinee in less than an hour," he said before hustling to his car.

"They're doing the show today?" I asked incredulously as we watched Norman climb into a white Cadillac. "I assumed they would wait a few days, at least."

"The show must go on," Mark said grandly.

"To be fair," Damien said, "the Sanctuary was open the night after you found Jared's body there. At least, that's what I hear."

That had happened just a couple of days before Damien had arrived to run the Sanctuary in his father's absence. It had taken a murder to convince him to return to Nightmare.

"I really need to tour this haunted house of yours," Mark said. "From what I hear, Damien, your house is even bigger than the one Olivia and I had in Nashville!"

I wondered if the two men could hear me grinding my teeth.

I announced I had marketing work to get done for the motel, said a curt goodbye to Mark, and walked to the car as quickly as I could without looking like I was fleeing the scene. Damien caught up to me just as I reached his car. When we climbed in, I shut the door with a bang.

To my utter surprise, Damien started to laugh. He bent his head over the steering wheel, his shoulders shaking in his mirth.

"What's so funny?" I snapped.

"You!" Damien sat up and sucked in a breath as he fought to get his laughter under control. "Is this what I get like? Do I have that same look on my face, as if the whole world has done me wrong? Be careful, or you'll start throwing things with your mind, too!"

I couldn't help but smile at Damien recognizing a bit of his own attitude in my behavior, but it was a good reminder that I needed to calm down. I forced my shoulders to relax and rolled them backward. "I'm sorry," I said honestly. "It's bad enough Mark had to show up here, but for him to make references to our life in Nashville, like everything there was sunshine and roses, really irks me. He's coming off as so fake."

"Has he always been like that?"

"Officer Reyes asked me the same thing. I don't think so. This Mark two-point-oh is doing everything he can to get back on his feet, and that seems to include acting like a slimy salesman." I gave Damien a teasing smile. "Judging by those water glasses, you didn't like his behavior any more than I did."

Damien looked down, and I thought I saw just the hint of red in his cheeks. "I felt your conjuring," he said at last. "There was this feeling"—Damien brought the tip of one finger to his temple—"like something was nudging on my brain, and the word *calm* popped into my thoughts."

My mouth fell open. My conjuring had really, truly worked on Damien.

Damien looked at me with a smile. A real one, not a fake one like Mark had taken a liking to. "Great job, Olivia. I'm proud of you."

It was my turn to blush. "If it weren't for you, I'd still think I was a normal person. Thanks for helping me learn all of this." I changed the subject abruptly, saying, "I think we need to talk to both Laura and Leo. Would you like to come with me?"

"Not yet. I had a text message from Mama, and she's asked us to collect Tanner and McCrory." Damien started his car and began to carefully back out of the parking spot.

"Are we taking them on a field trip?"

"We're taking them to the playground."

I laughed, but Damien looked totally serious. "Wait, really?" I asked.

"Lucy gets out of school in an hour. We're going to meet her and Mama at the school playground in the hope that our ghosts can establish communication with Lucy's ghost."

"Oh, brilliant idea!" It really was. Why hadn't I thought of that? If the ghosts of the outlaw and the sheriff could chat with the girl Lucy was seeing on the playground, it might help Lucy get some answers about why the girl kept appearing to her.

Tanner and McCrory's six-shooters were kept in a wooden box with a silver latch. The box was beat up and looked to be nearly as old as the guns themselves, which dated to the late eighteen hundreds. Damien drove us to the Sanctuary, and we went to his office so he could retrieve the box from one of his locked desk drawers. Since the ghosts were tethered to their guns, we had to bring the box along any time we wanted to take the ghosts somewhere.

As soon as Damien lifted the box out of the drawer, the two ghosts appeared, sending a cold wave of air through the room. "Do you require our services?" McCrory asked.

Damien nodded. "Yes. I'll explain in the car."

"Yeehaw! We're goin' out!" Tanner lifted his cowboy hat and waved it in the air.

Damien and I explained Lucy's situation as we drove. Tanner and McCrory were in the back, but since it was daytime, their forms were nearly invisible. Driving ghosts around was something I was still getting accustomed to, even though this was far from the first time I'd been in a car with the pair.

Since we had some time to kill before school got out for

the day, Damien treated the ghosts to a bit of a cruise around town. He took them past some of the newer buildings they hadn't seen yet, then he turned onto a two-lane road that wound up into the hills. "Hang on, boys," Damien said as he stomped on the gas pedal.

The road was twisty, and even though Damien expertly guided the car around the tight turns, I still had a death grip on the armrest. Behind me, though, both Tanner and McCrory were shouting their approval. *Someday,* I told myself, *we need to take them on a roller coaster.*

We eventually circled back and headed to the elementary school. Most of the students appeared to be gone already, and there were just a handful of cars waiting to pick kids up. We parked and headed for the playground at one side of the school. Unlike the rest of the campus, it wasn't fenced, so kids could play on it even when school wasn't in session. Lucy was on a swing, and Mama was perched on the edge of a slightly tilting merry-go-round.

Lucy slowed the swing down until it was low enough that she could leap out of the seat. "Hey, ghosts!" she yelled as she ran toward us.

"Good to see you again, little lady! Let's say howdy to this friend of yours." McCrory was just a shimmer as he swept toward Lucy. The ghost girl, on the other hand, had been materializing so clearly in the daylight that Lucy had originally thought she was a living person. Why was she so solid-looking? It was yet another mystery to solve.

Lucy stared at a spot in the air. "Ghost girl, I brought some friends for you to meet. They can help you."

After several more invitations, Lucy sighed. "I don't see her."

"I don't, either," I heard Tanner say from somewhere behind me. "I don't sense her presence at all. It looks like she's not here right now."

Lucy's shoulders slumped. "Sorry I made you two come out here for nothing."

McCrory laughed. "Don't be sorry! We've had a great time. Damien took us for a drive, and his car sure beats any stagecoach I ever rode in."

Tanner and McCrory began to tell Lucy about Damien's driving skills as I gazed around the playground. The chain-link fence that surrounded the school ran along one side of it. "How could coyotes have gotten inside the corral unless someone let them in through the gate?" I mused.

I had been talking to myself, but Damien overheard me. "A better question is, why was Billy in the corral in the first place? It was nighttime."

"Maybe he was there to meet someone in secret."

Damien looked at me grimly. "Someone who came ready to kill."

CHAPTER THIRTEEN

The playground ghost was obviously not going to show up, so there was no point sticking around. I caught a ride with Mama, since we were both returning to the motel, while Damien took Tanner and McCrory back to the Sanctuary.

Lucy was disappointed not to have communicated with the ghost, but her excitement about seeing Tanner and McCrory again made up for it. She talked about them the entire drive back to the motel, running through everything they had said to her on the playground, even though Mama and I had been right there to witness it.

I followed Mama and Lucy into the office once we were back at the motel. Lucy had finally calmed down, and she settled into one of the chairs as Mama headed for her desk behind the counter.

"I need your help," I said in a low voice, leaning my elbows on the counter. "You told me a woman who checked in here said she's a part of the stunt show. I'd like to have a chat with her."

Mama gave me a look that was both stern and apologetic. "You know I can't give out guest information. Yes, we did it that one time, but that was different, because those guests were murder suspects. People trust us to keep their information private."

Right, of course. I had forgotten that rule. "What can you tell me, then?"

"She's tall and thin, and she looks like she lives half of her life in a tanning bed. Her hair is bleached so much it's a wonder it hasn't all broken off, and it hits about here." Mama put the edge of her hand against her sternum.

I thanked Mama for the intel, then made my way back to my apartment. It was time for my first stakeout. I dragged one of my chairs onto the concrete landing outside my door and settled into it.

I quickly got bored, and I looked at my watch impatiently. I had only been sitting there for fifteen minutes. In that time, I hadn't seen a single person come or go as I looked out over the parking lot.

The time passed a lot more quickly once I had a book in my hands. I would read a bit, glance up, then return to reading. Still, there just wasn't a lot happening at Cowboy's Corral. I saw a couple come out of a room with their two young children in tow, and Benny wandered past at one point with a toolbox in his hand. He waved at me and hollered a hello. Judging by his sly smile, he knew exactly what I was doing.

The time was nearing when I would have to get ready for work that night, and I was about to give up when a room door in the wing opposite the parking lot opened up, and a tall, tan woman emerged. Her bleach-blond hair was pulled back in a high ponytail.

Without stopping to think about what I should do, I threw my book onto the ground, bolted out of my chair, and raced down the steps. It was only as I was hurrying toward the woman, who was walking up to a gray sedan with keys in her hand, that I realized I must look like some kind of stalker. I slowed my pace and waved. "Excuse me?"

The woman paused and looked at me warily. "What?"

"I live in the apartment up there," I said, gesturing

over my shoulder. "Mama—one of the owners of the motel—mentioned there was someone staying here who was connected to the stunt show. Is it you?"

The woman's eyes narrowed. She was wearing a thick layer of black eyeliner, which made her look slightly villainous. "Why are you asking?"

My first instinct was to feel taken aback by the woman's coldness, but then I realized that if our positions were reversed, I would be reacting the same way. I wasn't coming off as friendly, and I said self-consciously, "Sorry. I'm going about this all wrong. Mama mentioned you have a connection to the show, and since I do, too, I wanted to introduce myself."

"Connection?" The woman gave a sniff of disapproval. "The new *star*"—her voice dripped with sarcasm on the word—"is my ex-husband. I came here to make sure I get the money he owes me."

I laughed at that, which only made the woman look even more uncomfortable. Mama and I had joked that the new guest was probably someone's ex, but I hadn't really expected it to be true. "You and I are in a similar situation, then," I explained. "My ex-husband is Trent's manager."

"Oh, you used to be married to that guy? Boy, you and I need to go to the saloon and dish over a glass or two of wine." The woman relaxed and held out a hand. "Stacy Nash."

"Olivia Kendrick," I said, shaking Stacy's hand while noting she hadn't gone back to her maiden name, like I had. "And yes, we should definitely compare notes."

"Did you also drive out here from Nashville to keep an eye on your ex?"

"No. I've been living here since August, in fact. I was shocked when Mark suddenly showed up."

Stacy nodded sagely. "He apparently got wind that the show here was looking for some young new talent. After

Trent got fired from the show in Nashville, I thought I'd never get my money, so when he told me he was starting this gig, I was all for it."

"He got fired?" I asked. I remembered Trent telling me he had left because he didn't like the show's new direction.

"Oh, yeah. Trent's ego kept getting in the way, so they axed him. His ego ruined our marriage, too. It's a theme with him."

After what I had seen during Trent's costume fitting, I wasn't about to disagree.

Stacy and I definitely had some things in common, though I thought it was a bit extreme that she had followed her ex-husband all the way from Tennessee to Arizona just so she could keep an eye on him and his finances. I wasn't sure if Stacy was a suspect or someone who deserved my sympathy.

Maybe she was both.

With that in mind, I told her we should make good on that glass of wine soon. "I work at night," I told her, "but I have Mondays off. Maybe after the weekend?"

Stacy lifted her hand in a salute. "See you at the saloon. Oh, and if you need anything, I'm in room thirty-one."

I pointed to my front door. "Second floor on the corner. See you soon."

I headed back to my apartment, feeling proud of my successful stakeout. There wasn't much time for me to celebrate, though, since I had to get ready for work. I changed into black jeans and my black Nightmare Sanctuary Haunted House T-shirt, then ran a brush through my hair and touched up my makeup. Since the weather was nice, I wanted to walk, so I pulled on my lightweight coat and headed out.

Only halfway to the Sanctuary, I heard a growl and froze instantly. After what had happened to Billy, I was picturing a coyote lurking behind the nearby plants, just waiting to attack. There was a flash of movement, and something launched through the underbrush toward me. I sucked in my breath and started to run, even as I realized there was nothing to be afraid of.

"Zach, you jerk!" I shouted at the werewolf.

Zach sat back on his haunches, looking incredibly proud of himself.

"It's not funny!" I continued.

Felipe came bounding out from behind a prickly pear cactus. He ran up to me, rose onto his back legs, and pressed his paws against my thighs. I patted his leathery gray head. "I'm not mad at you." I looked at Zach. "Come on. We need to get to the family meeting."

Zach rose and padded along beside me as I continued down the road. Felipe ran around us, sometimes darting off the road, presumably in search of a snack. It was a surreal feeling to have a werewolf and a chupacabra escorting me to work, but it was also nice. I felt safe.

When I got to the front doors of the Sanctuary, I opened one of them and stepped back to let my two companions through. It was barely dark, but Mori was already coming up the stairs from the basement, where she and Theo had their windowless apartments.

"Felipe, there you are!" Mori's floor-length purple gown rustled as she walked over to him. Then, she looked at Zach. "Has he been behaving?"

I figured that was a polite way of asking if Felipe had been drinking the blood of any local livestock, as chupacabras tended to do. Zach dipped his snout and huffed out a breath, which Mori took as a *yes*. The cows of Nightmare were safe, at least for the moment.

Mori and I chatted as we headed for the dining room. "How are you doing?" she asked gently. "It's got to be awkward having your ex in town, especially when you and Damien…"

"When me and Damien, what?" I asked, giving her a sidelong glance.

Mori didn't answer. She just gave me a wicked smile.

During the family meeting, Justine announced I would be stationed at the entrance, taking tickets. No sooner had I gone up to the front doors to take up my post than Zach came up. He looked from me to the door, then back at me. "Do you want to go out?" I asked. "Again?"

Zach whimpered, so I opened the door and let him out. *Is he my co-worker or my pet dog?*

I had just let in the first guests of the night when Zach returned, trotting past a family and through the door. The parents looked worried, but the kids started bouncing with excitement. "He's so cute!" the daughter squeaked. It probably wasn't the reaction Zach had been hoping for.

After I let in the final guests of the evening, Malcolm closed the ticket window and joined me in the entryway. "We're taking you to Under the Undertaker's tonight," he said as we watched the last group in the queue enter the door to the haunt. "Mori told me during my break. She says you've earned a drink."

"She's not wrong."

Theo and Mori went by us about ten minutes later. Mori was heading downstairs to change out of her gown, and Theo was on his way to the costume room to take off his pirate getup. Before long, both of them had rejoined us. Theo never got all of his black eyeliner off, and he reminded me of Stacy Nash. *Maybe she used to be a pirate, too,* I thought.

"Mori, have I earned a drink because I'm trying to find Billy's killer, or because Mark is in town?" I asked.

"Both, of course." Mori had changed into a low-cut

black dress that fit her tightly. She definitely put the "vamp" in vampire.

There was a loud bang behind me, and I turned to see Gunnar running through the front door. "Oh, good, you're still here," he said to me breathlessly.

"What's wrong?" I asked, instantly alert.

"Not wrong, exactly, but I have some curious news to share. I've been wanting to fly over the corral, more out of curiosity than anything else. As soon as we closed for the night, I took off. When I got over to the stunt show, I dropped as low as I dared—I didn't want anyone there to spot me—and I saw something moving in the corral."

"What kind of something?" Theo asked.

Gunnar shook his head. "I don't know, but it wasn't a human, and it wasn't a horse. If an animal was involved in Billy's murder, then I think it's back, and it was somehow able to get through the corral fence."

I felt a shiver work its way up my spine. "Or someone let it in."

CHAPTER FOURTEEN

"What kind of animal are we talking about?" Theo asked. He began moving toward the door, like he was going to head to the corral to investigate right that very moment, but Mori grabbed his sleeve to stop him.

"I don't know," Gunnar said. "I was too high to see any detail, but it was too small to be a horse."

"Could it have been a coyote, like the police have speculated?" I was mentally seeing the corral in my mind and wondering where there might be an undiscovered break in the wooden fence.

Gunnar shrugged, his large, sinewy wings rising and falling with the movement. "Maybe, though if I had to guess, I'd say it was a little too large to be a coyote. They tend to be scrawny things."

"Unless there's another clawed-up body in the morning, I'm going to guess it's a critter that found an entrance into the corral," I said. "I don't think the killer would be dumb enough to go back to the scene of the crime to strike again."

"In the meantime," Mori said, "let's continue this conversation at the bar. Unless we're all willing to run out to the stunt show right now to take a closer look, there's no reason to delay getting our drinks."

Everyone nodded in agreement. Although, once we

arrived at the bar, we didn't continue the conversation. Instead, we fell into our usual habit of talking about our night at work. Under the Undertaker's was a hidden bar for supernaturals, accessible by a nondescript door in an alleyway behind High Noon Boulevard. While we were there, Clara and Justine came in, and we waved them over to sit with us.

"Olivia, how are you holding up?" Clara asked. "My sister and I just returned from driving my grandparents back to their house in Albuquerque, and I hear your ex is in town."

I threw my hands up in mock exasperation. "Does everyone in this town know?"

Clara grinned at me, her violet eyes sparkling with humor. "The messenger posted at the city limits filled us in."

"Ha-ha," I intoned.

Clara giggled and gestured toward the bar. "You can't really be surprised. My family owns this place, and bars are the best place to hear the latest news. Plus, fairies love gossip. I knew before we hit the road back here."

I could only shake my head in wonder that word got around Nightmare so quickly. We soon moved past the subject, though, as we began to ask Clara for details about her trip. And, as we talked, I looked around the bar, which was lit by candles that flickered off the long swaths of material hanging from the ceiling. The jewel-toned hangings created cozy spaces around the low tables.

At least Mark won't unexpectedly show up here, I thought. He would never get past the fairy working the door.

The night turned out to be exactly what I needed. There was no chance of running into Mark, and since Damien wasn't there, I didn't have to worry he would get upset and start flinging wine glasses across the bar with his mind.

It was just a fun night out with my friends.

I woke up on Friday morning not with my friends on my mind, but suspects. Norman and Trent were still at the top of my list, though Stacy was certainly one for me to keep an eye on, too. Even though I could relate to her situation, I couldn't overlook the fact that she really, really wanted Trent to make money so she could get her share of it.

There was also Leo Whitehall, the former horse trainer for the stunt show. Norman had been quick to say Leo was retired these days, but Mark had made it sound like that retirement hadn't been Leo's choice. It was time to talk to him to find out the truth.

When I had gone looking for information online about Leo before, I had found some references to his work but nothing to indicate how to track him down. That meant it was time to go the old-fashioned route: I headed to the motel office and asked Mama for the phone book. I couldn't remember the last time I had flipped through one of those, but it was exactly what I needed. Within minutes, I had Leo's address and phone number.

Mama suggested I call first, but I decided this was a conversation that needed to happen in person. And, if I called first and explained to Leo why I wanted to meet with him, he might refuse. I didn't want to think of my visit to him as a sneak attack, but that was really what it was.

Leo's house wasn't far from the stunt show. In fact, the two places were on the same two-lane road, separated by only about three miles. As I pulled into the long, dirt drive that led to a modest one-story house, I realized how easy it would have been for Leo to run over to the stunt show, murder Billy, and get back home before anyone knew what had happened.

The house looked like it was at least a hundred years old, and the green paint on the wooden clapboard exterior was faded and peeling. There were tall trees planted on the sides of the house, which would provide ample shade in the summertime.

I pulled up and climbed out of the car, suddenly second-guessing myself. I couldn't ring the doorbell and ask Leo if he had murdered someone. Luckily, there was another route I could take.

I waited so long after ringing the doorbell that I was about to turn and leave, when the door cracked open a few inches. "Yes?" said a raspy male voice.

"Leo?" I guessed. "Hi. I'm Olivia Kendrick. You don't know me, but my ex-husband is working with the stunt show now, and, well, I was hoping we could talk."

"Your ex, huh?"

"Yes, he's my ex, but I want to make sure he's okay. He's trying really hard to get back on his feet."

Leo gave a long, low laugh, then opened the door wide. He wasn't as old as Norman had implied, but he did have deep-set crow's feet that crinkled around his faded blue eyes as he said, "You sound just like that Nash woman! She came around yesterday, looking for the same kind of information. How many ex-wives does this new guy have?"

"I was married to Trent Nash's manager," I clarified.

"Mm-hmm. Let me guess: you want to make sure this job will pay enough that some of it winds up in your pocket, too? You're after your alimony?"

I stammered and sputtered at Leo's direct questioning, and he seemed to take it as confirmation that this was, in fact, all about the money. He laughed again and stepped back. "Come on in. I'll do my best to reassure you."

Leo led me into a living room that looked like a time capsule from the nineteen eighties, right down to the sagging brown sectional that took up most of the room. I sat down and gazed at the floral wallpaper, which was nearly hidden by all the photos of horses.

"All of these were mine," Leo said proudly as he sat. "I didn't own them, but I trained them. Some of them went on to be in the stunt show, of course."

"They're all beautiful animals," I commented.

"Thank you. You should see the Quarter horse I'm training right now out at Jonathan Wilkes's ranch. One of the most beautiful, intelligent horses I've had the pleasure of working with."

"You're still training horses, then? Norman had mentioned you retired."

Leo snorted derisively. "Retired? Of course not. I have bills to pay! Norman is probably trying to make himself feel better by claiming I retired."

I peered at Leo. "Why would he need to make himself feel better?"

"Because I'm a great trainer, and he knows it. But Billy decided he didn't like me, and he raised a fuss until Norman agreed to get rid of me."

"I only met Billy once, and it was brief, but I get the impression he was a bit of a hothead."

"You could say that." Leo leaned back and crossed his legs. He stared toward a photo of two horses galloping next to each other, but I could tell by his glazed expression that he wasn't seeing them. "Billy had a big ego and a bad temper, and those two things together caused some real trouble. He started getting lax with his own training, and I warned him that he was going to endanger himself and the horses. Billy hated being criticized, so he tried to turn it around on me. He started claiming I wasn't taking proper care of the horses."

I looked around, again, at all the horse photos on the walls. Leo clearly loved his profession. "I'm guessing you gave those horses excellent care."

"Of course I did. But Billy wouldn't back off, especially when I'd be brushing the horses after the nighttime show, and he'd come into the barn drunk. What did he know about caring for horses, anyway? He was born with a silver spoon in his mouth, and he never once had to take care of the horses he was riding."

"A silver spoon?" I repeated.

"Sure. Billy had family money, which is how he could afford to be a stunt rider without half-starving to death. It's not a lucrative career, unless you're with one of the big-time shows." Leo seemed to sense my interest, and he got a self-satisfied look as he slowed down and said dramatically, "Billy never got married or had any kids, so rumor has it that whatever's left of the family fortune will go directly to the stunt show."

I couldn't hide my look of surprise. That bit of news, if true, was just more motive for Norman. Not only would killing Billy pave the way for a new star and a revitalized show, but it would also mean a nice influx of cash to help the show's allegedly troubled finances.

Leo mistook my expression, and he added, "Yes, that money will make sure the new guy gets his payday, and his manager, too. Those two are in a nice spot, and you're going to have no problem getting your alimony."

"It sounds like Billy was tough to work with, but what about the others? Is Norman a decent guy?"

"The man fired me, so I'm not the right one to ask. Before that, though, I never had any complaints."

I nodded and stood. "Thank you for your time, Leo. I really appreciate it."

"Always happy to help. I've had two pretty women stop by in the past two days. The neighbors are going to talk!" Leo chuckled to himself as he rose and led the way to the front door.

I thanked Leo again as I stepped out into the sunshine. Right before I could say goodbye, I heard loud barking to my left. Two large dogs were running toward me.

I shrank back, and Leo shouted, "Bomber! Biplane! Hush, now!" He looked at me apologetically. "So sorry if they scared you. They're supposed to be in the west paddock, but they can wiggle through even the tiniest little gap in the fence. Don't worry. They won't hurt you unless I tell them to!"

CHAPTER FIFTEEN

The dogs had slowed to a walk when Leo called to them, and they ambled up to me with their long legs. The first one, whom I presumed was Bomber, nearly came up to my waist.

Gunnar said the animal he spotted looked bigger than a coyote.

And, if these dogs were good at worming their way through gaps in fences, then maybe one or both of them had been responsible for attacking Billy.

Leo had good reason to dislike Billy, and if his dogs attacked on command, then I really had to consider that Leo was the murderer. Maybe he had referenced Billy's family money going to the show to shift suspicion onto Norman. Maybe he and Norman were in on it together, and they were going to split the money.

Maybe I should leave, right now.

My heart was still pounding, even as I assured Leo the dogs had only startled me a bit. One of them licked my hand while I said that, and I rubbed the back of my hand against my jeans to remove the copious amount of drool. "Thank you, again," I said. "Have a nice day."

The dogs and Leo both disappeared inside the house as I got into my car and turned around in the small circular space at the end of the drive. I breathed a sigh of relief as I approached the road, and I mentally chastised myself for going alone to the home of someone who might have committed murder just a few days before.

I wasn't any closer to knowing who had killed Billy, but Mark was looking less and less likely as the culprit. That made me feel better, at least, since proving his innocence was the whole reason I had started looking into Billy's death in the first place.

Instead of driving right back to the motel, I headed for The Lusty Lunch Counter. It was a bit early for lunch, but I figured I deserved a cheeseburger and fries. The dogs had scared me much more than I had admitted to Leo, since I had thought of Gunnar's report the moment I had seen them careening toward me. My favorite lunch seemed like the right thing to soothe my nerves.

By the time I had a belly full of food and had enjoyed chatting with my friend and usual server, Ella, I was feeling more settled. Whether or not Leo and his dogs were guilty, no harm had come to me, and he hadn't even known my visit was a chance to investigate Billy's murder.

I spent the afternoon in the motel office, working on the laptop Mama had loaned me while occasionally stopping to chat with her. At one point, I looked outside and realized the sun was getting close to the horizon. I had been so caught up in writing a description of the motel for an Arizona travel guide that I had totally lost track of the time. "I gotta go!" I yelped.

Mama grinned at me. "Somebody's excited to see her co-workers."

"More like I'm running out of time to change clothes and get ready." I wished Mama a good night and hustled back to my apartment. Once I was in a fresh Nightmare Sanctuary T-shirt, I sped through my routine of touching up my hair and face. I walked out of my apartment only four minutes later than my usual time, so I relaxed a bit. I would arrive with time to spare if I drove instead of walking.

I wound up having just enough extra time to duck into Damien's office when I arrived. There had been times in the past when his office had felt heavy or even electrified, like the state of his mind changed the atmosphere around him. On this night, Damien's office felt light and welcoming.

"Good evening," I said as Damien looked up.

"Yes, it is," he answered brightly.

It was almost unnerving to see Damien looking so happy.

"I just finished reviewing the numbers for October, which Zach wrapped up right before the full moon." Damien lifted a stack of papers on his desk and gave them a shake. "It was a very good month."

"I'm glad to hear it." When Damien had first arrived in Nightmare, he had claimed one reason for taking over his father's business had been to right its finances. He had felt like the Sanctuary wasn't in as good of shape as it should have been.

I chatted with Damien for a few minutes, enjoying this content, smiling version of him. It was a side of Damien I wouldn't mind seeing a lot more of, and I knew once he worked his way past his anger and resentment toward Baxter—and once he learned more about his power and how to control it—Damien had the potential to be a great guy. He'd already improved a lot since the first time I had met him.

That night, I was in the lagoon vignette once again. Seraphina decided she wanted to get in on the competition Theo and I had going with each other. Before we opened to guests, she swam to the top of the water tank, which sat next to a prop pirate ship.

"I'm not just a pretty face, you know," she called down

to us. She propped her elbows on the edge of the tank and rested her chin on her arms. Her skin had a green sheen to it, but there was no arguing with Seraphina that she was pretty. "I want in on the game. Even though I can't chase after guests like you two can, I bet I can scare someone so bad that they sprint out of this vignette."

Theo raised an eyebrow at Seraphina. "How quickly do you think you can do this?"

Seraphina looked thoughtful for a moment. "Within the first fifty guests."

Theo looked at me. "You keep count of the guests, and I'll judge whether someone is running or simply walking hastily."

"Oh, they're going to run," Seraphina said confidently.

It was guest number thirty-four. The party of six walked into the vignette with their arms tightly around each other, except for one young man who walked at the back of the group, smirking. Clearly, he was laughing at his friends' fear.

Seraphina's tank faced away from my usual spot, but I saw the guy walk toward her, his face slack. I didn't want to start laughing and ruin the effect of our creepy scene for anyone, so I bit my lip as I watched. I didn't know how sirens lured men, but Seraphina must have been doing it at that moment. The man began to take off his jacket, as if he were going to climb into the tank and swim with her.

Briefly, the man disappeared from my view as he moved to stand closer to the front of Seraphina's tank. He reappeared just a few seconds later, shrieking as he elbowed his way past his friends and shot right past me into the hallway that led to the next vignette. Startled, his friends hurried after him, calling his name.

I couldn't hold in my laughter anymore. I bent double as tears formed in my eyes, and I heard Seraphina call out, "I told you two I could do it!"

By the time the Sanctuary closed at midnight, I was in a great mood. Damien was happy, the Sanctuary's finances were looking good, and I'd had a fun night with my friends. I told Gunnar as much when I ran into him in the hallway after I had changed out of my pirate costume.

"It's your haircut," Gunnar assured me. "It looks so good that you can't help but have more fun."

"That's what it is," I assured him with a wink.

Gunnar reached out a hand and touched the ends of my hair. "Next time, maybe I should try— Zach? What's wrong?"

I followed Gunnar's gaze and saw Zach running toward us. He stopped in front of me and whined, his eyes wide and staring at my face.

"Is something wrong?" I asked him.

Zach whimpered, then growled.

"I think that's a *yes*," Gunnar said.

"I wish he could tell us about it."

Zach ran a circle around Gunnar and me, then stared up at me again. When I told him I didn't know what to do, he ran two more circles around us, then turned his head toward the end of the hallway.

"I think he wants us to follow him," Gunnar said. Zach yipped in answer, and Gunnar nodded. "Go ahead. We're right behind you."

Zach yipped again, then ran to the dining room door and scratched at it. I opened it for him, and he dashed inside. By the time I was through the door, too, I could see Zach was standing next to a table, where Fiona was shuffling cards. "You joining the poker game?" she called to me in her husky voice.

"We're following Zach," I explained.

Zach shook his head, his jowls flapping with the movement, then headed toward the hallway again. Gunnar and

I followed him to the entryway. Malcolm had just come down the stairs, and Zach began to run circles around him.

"Zach wants you to follow him," I explained as Malcolm stared in confusion at Zach. "He did the same thing to us."

"I think he was looking for you in the dining room," Gunnar added. "He expected you to be at Fiona's poker game. Apparently, he wants you to join us."

Malcolm strode to the entrance and pulled both doors open. "Let's go!"

Zach shot outside with Malcolm and Gunnar on his heels. Keeping up with a werewolf, a wendigo, and a gargoyle, as it turned out, wasn't easy to do. Not only did Malcolm have incredible speed, but both he and Gunnar towered over me. They outpaced me quickly as they chased after Zach.

We were almost to the gallows before anyone seemed to realize I was lagging behind. I was jogging along and already breathing hard.

"I'm not old enough to be this out of shape," I huffed to myself.

Gunnar called out to Zach, and the three of them stood at the crossroads to wait for me. With the old wooden gallows gleaming in the light of the full moon, it made for an eerie tableau.

"Zach, I'm not as fast as you," I said after I had caught my breath.

Zach made a yip that I took as acknowledgment, and when he started moving again, he was going slower so I could keep up.

We walked briskly for about ten more minutes, and every now and then, Zach would dart forward, then turn and wait for me to get close to him again. He seemed to be impatient to get to wherever he was leading us.

Eventually, we were on a narrow dirt road that ran

between an overgrown field on one side and a wild area full of trees and boulders on the other. Zach slowed his pace as we walked down the road, and his nose was nearly on the ground.

Malcolm sniffed loudly. "I'm getting a whiff of whatever Zach smells. It could be a coyote, maybe a wolf. Some kind of dog, at any rate."

I thought of Leo Whitehall's two dogs. How far were we from his house? Had they snuck through the fence and gone for a midnight walk along this same road?

Even as I was wondering that, a form that was much bigger than Bomber or Biplane darted across the road. We all froze, except for Zach, who lurched forward with a growl.

The creature, whatever it was, had disappeared behind a huge boulder, but a loud snarl cut through the air. There was the sound of something trampling over dry plants and tree branches, and then a shadowy form emerged from the underbrush.

I didn't get a good look before muscular arms wrapped around me tightly. My own arms were pinned to my sides.

Even as I felt panic rising inside me, I looked down and recognized Gunnar's hands. Or paws. I still wasn't sure what to call them.

"Zach, get out of here!" Malcolm yelled. "Run!" He took his own advice, turning and clearing the low fence that bordered the field in one graceful jump. He shot into the darkness, and I saw Zach following in his wake.

There was another snarl, and I turned in the direction of the mysterious creature right as my feet left the ground. Gunnar's wings made a loud *whoosh* with every beat, and the creature grew smaller as we rose higher in the air.

CHAPTER SIXTEEN

I didn't know whether to be scared or excited. I was worried about Malcolm and Zach, and I was also very aware that my feet were dangling below me, and the ground was steadily getting farther away.

At the same time, though, I was flying! There was something thrilling about the feel of the cold night air whipping against my face, and I was grateful Gunnar had been able to so easily pluck me out of a dangerous situation.

While he and I were out of danger, Zach and Malcolm were having to rely on their supernatural speed to get away from whatever that looming form had been. Gunnar seemed to be thinking the same thing, because he stopped moving upward and began to fly forward, following our friends across the field.

I let out a nervous squeak when Gunnar suddenly dipped lower, and he grumbled in my ear, "You're safe, Olivia. I just want to keep close to Zach and Malcolm."

"We need to get back to the Sanctuary," I shouted over the sound of the wind. I looked toward the horizon, and I could see a long, straight row of streetlights. That, I knew, was the road Cowboy's Corral was on, so the cluster of low lights near it had to be High Noon Boulevard.

Once I had oriented myself, I twisted my head around

as much as I could and said, "Direct them to the mine! It's closer!"

"The one Damien is living in? But you told us it's warded against werewolves! Zach can't get in."

"I have a plan," I assured him.

Gunnar swooped even lower, until we were only a few feet off the ground. I bent my knees for fear my toes might hit a rock. Flying, I quickly realized, got more scary the lower we went. Gunnar was just behind Malcolm, and he shouted, "Follow me!"

With that, Gunnar rose—much to my relief—and speeded ahead. He knew where the mine was, and in just a couple of minutes, Gunnar landed gracefully right in front of the iron door that led inside the rock face.

The second Gunnar let go of my arms, I dashed forward and started to bang on the door. "Damien, it's me! We need help!"

I heard loud footsteps, and a moment later, the rusty door squealed open. Damien's hand shot out, and he grabbed my arm and began to pull me inside.

"No, your car! I need your car keys!" I said, resisting his attempt to pull me to safety.

Damien's eyebrows knit together, but he didn't stop to question my bizarre request. He wordlessly reached into his pocket and pulled out his keyring.

"Damien, let's go!" I insisted. I ran to Damien's car, unlocked it, and opened the passenger-side door. Malcolm and Zach were already running up, and I called to Zach, who jumped inside. Malcolm yanked open the other door and curled his tall frame into the back.

"I'll meet you at the Sanctuary," Gunnar called. He kicked up a cloud of dust as he beat his wings and rose into the air, and I coughed.

Damien was already sliding into the driver's seat, and I leaned into the passenger side. "Get in the back," I told

Zach, pushing against his haunches. It was a squeeze, but he managed to wiggle his way between the seats. He and Malcolm would be cramped in the back, but it was a short drive.

Once I had the door shut, I looked out the window, but there was no sign of the creature. Malcolm and I filled Damien in as he drove us to the Sanctuary. He was taking the turns alarmingly fast, but after flying through the air with Gunnar, it didn't seem all that scary.

Damien pulled his car right up to the front doors of the Sanctuary. The circular drive was cracked and choked with weeds, so it was a bumpy ride. The four of us hustled out of the car, and we found Gunnar waiting for us.

Once we were all inside the entryway, Malcolm locked the doors and turned to us. "Like I said earlier," he told us calmly, "I can't smell the difference between dog breeds. However, that form on the road was definitely canine."

"I've never seen a dog that big in my life," I said. My legs started to feel wobbly as the adrenaline drained out of me, so I walked over to the staircase and plopped down onto the bottom step.

"Yes, you have," Gunnar said. He pointed at Zach.

"You think it was a werewolf you encountered?" Damien asked.

Zach yipped loudly in answer.

"I think it's very likely," Malcolm translated.

"I had just gotten back to the mine," Damien said to me. "You're lucky I was there."

"Yes and no," I answered. "We thought we were in danger, but I don't know that the creature was giving chase. I think we might have scared it as much as it scared us."

"It was four against one," Gunnar pointed out. "Plus, if I ran into me on a dark road in the middle of the night, I'd be scared, too." To drive home his point, he flexed his shoulders, his muscular chest puffing out and his wings expanding slightly.

"I think it's safe to say this creature is the same one you saw earlier tonight in the stunt show corral," I noted.

"Yes, the size was right," Gunnar said. "Bigger than a coyote, but smaller than a horse. That still leaves us with the question of how it got into the corral, and whether or not it's the creature responsible for Billy's death."

Malcolm leaned against a door and crossed his arms. "It also raises the question of whether Billy really was murdered, or if the animal attack theory is correct, after all. Whether the creature was a werewolf or not, Billy's demise may not have been intentional."

I sighed. "Our list of questions continues to grow longer. Will someone please remind me why I felt the need to get involved with this case to begin with?"

"To prove your ex-husband's innocence," Damien said. I thought I detected a hint of disdain in his voice.

"Right." I propped my chin in my hands. "And now we have a possibly supernatural creature on our suspect list."

"All the more reason for you to continue investigating, Olivia." Malcolm moved toward me and held out a hand. When I took it, he pulled me to my feet. "We need to know who or what we saw tonight, even if the creature wasn't involved in Billy's murder."

"In the meantime," Damien said, "there's nothing more we can do tonight, unless you're planning to put together a hunting party."

"We're not going to hunt this thing!" I said, horrified.

"I didn't mean it literally." Damien looked at me. "But I don't want anything hunting you, either. I'll drive you home."

"No need. My car is out front."

"Then I'll follow you back to your apartment. I know how good you are at getting into trouble, and I want to see you walk inside and shut your door before I'll be satisfied you're safe."

"I don't get myself into that much trouble," I protested. Gunnar, Malcolm, and Damien all snickered at that.

Gunnar and Zach escorted me to my car while Malcolm stuck close to Damien. It was like we had a security detail. I wasn't worried we had been followed, though, and within a few short minutes, I was at the top of my stairs, waving down at Damien. He was true to his word: only after I had shut and locked my door behind me did I hear the rumble of his engine as he sped off.

I woke up on Saturday morning well before my alarm went off, so I rolled over and did my best to go back to sleep. The night's adventure felt like some kind of dream, and I wound up tossing and turning as I went over all the details in my mind. Eventually, I gave up and started my day.

My first order of business was coffee, but my second was having a chat with Mama. I wanted to get her opinion on what had happened, but I also wanted her to be on her guard. I didn't think the mysterious creature was going to pop into the motel office and ask about the room rate, but I did want her to keep an eye out when she headed home at night.

When I neared the front of the office, I was delighted to see a tow truck parked out front. Nick Dalton had rescued me the day my car broke down outside of Nightmare, and he was the one who had brought me to the motel, assuring me I'd get the "friends and family" discount since I had been short on cash. I would always be grateful to Mama and Benny's son for his kindness.

My joy grew even more when I walked inside the office, and the first thing I saw was Lucy, who was standing on top of one of the chairs. She seemed to be regaling her dad and grandmother with a story from school.

"And then I was like, 'You think *that* was a good presentation? Let me show you what *I* can do!'" she was saying. "I made everyone laugh when I talked about playing a zombie pirate, but then they screamed when they saw my scary face! Oh, hey, Miss Olivia!"

Lucy jumped off the chair and ran over to me. She hugged me around the waist and said in a stage whisper, "I need to talk to you."

"Okay. What's up?"

"Not here!" Lucy jerked her head in the direction of her dad, Nick. "We need to have some girl talk."

"Oh." I glanced at Mama, but she looked mystified, too. "Why don't we walk around the motel? We'll get some sunshine and exercise while we talk."

Lucy took my hand and led the way out the door while I promised Nick I'd catch up with him shortly.

Once we were outside, Lucy said, "I saw her again yesterday. She showed up next to the balance beam, and I asked her if she needed help."

"Did the ghost answer you this time?"

"She nodded her head, and then she disappeared. She needs my help, like you said!"

"You're making great progress," I assured Lucy. "You haven't met her yet, but there's a psychic medium at the Sanctuary named Vivian. I think it's time we ask her to assist."

"Cool. I hope I can help the ghost soon. She always looks so mean, but as she was disappearing, her face changed. She looked scared and sad."

"Maybe she's been putting on a brave face all this time, even though she really needs help."

And maybe, I thought to myself, *the creature we saw last night needs help, too.* As giant and frightening as it had looked, maybe it was as sad and scared as Lucy's ghost girl.

CHAPTER SEVENTEEN

Lucy began to detail what it would be like when she grew up and became a famous psychic medium. She said her mom sometimes watched reality TV shows that featured mediums, and maybe, someday, Lola would see her own daughter starring in one of them.

I added in the appropriate encouragement, but my mind wasn't really on Lucy's ambitious plans for her future. I was too busy wondering if the creature truly was in need of help. Like my mixed feelings toward Stacy Nash, I didn't know whether to feel suspicion or sympathy. It was very possible we had come face-to-face with the animal that had killed Billy, but it was also possible the attack had been self-defense.

There was just so much we didn't know, and there were so many suspects. And, as Malcolm had pointed out the night before, it was possible Billy had simply been killed in an animal attack, and no one had orchestrated it. Despite so many people having a motive, they could all be innocent, after all.

I felt a little hand on my arm. "Miss Olivia? Did you hear me?"

We had made it three-quarters of the way around the motel property, and I realized that, at some point, I had completely tuned out. I gave myself a shake and looked at

Lucy apologetically. "I'm sorry. I was in outer space. What did you say?"

"I said I'd really like to play with that dog again. The one your friend Mori owns."

"And I'm sure Felipe would be happy to play with you, too. In fact, if your dad says it's okay, how about you and me go to the Sanctuary right now? We can see if Felipe wants to go for a walk, and we can ask Maida to join us."

"Yay!" Lucy skipped all the way back to the office.

Nick was enthusiastic in giving his permission. "Lola's always packed with clients on Saturdays," he said, referring to his wife's work as a hair stylist. "Lucy was going to have to sit here or at my garage, and she'll be a lot happier getting out and about."

With that settled, Lucy and I drove over to the Sanctuary. The front doors were locked, which was typical during the day, so I knocked. It was Justine who answered, and she immediately high-fived Lucy. "Welcome back, pirate!" Justine enthused.

I left the two of them together in the entryway as I went in search of both Felipe and Maida. My first stop was the basement, where Mori and Theo had their apartments, and I called Felipe's name softly as I padded down the hallway. I wasn't sure if vampires could wake up during the day, but just in case, I didn't want to make too much noise.

There was no response to my calls, so I headed up to the second floor. Maida shared an apartment up there with Madge and Morgan. It was so cozy one would never guess it was a few hospital rooms that had been converted into a living space. Maida answered my knock, and no sooner had the words "Lucy is downstairs" come out of my mouth than she ran past me. Her lace-up black boots smacked against the concrete floor of the hallway as she raced toward the stairs.

I called Felipe's name again, and when I heard a snuffling sound, I turned to see him sitting in the middle of the hallway. I had no idea where he had come from. He was as good at sneaking around as Theo.

"Come on, Felipe. Let's go outside and play!" Like Maida, he reacted instantly, and soon, I was alone in the hallway.

By the time I came down the stairs, Maida and Lucy were already petting Felipe and cooing over how cute they both thought he was. I paused for a moment to appreciate the scene. It was good for both of the girls to make friends, and I knew Felipe was happy to be the means of their bonding.

I invited Justine to join us on our walk, but she said she had to get back to work. As soon as we were outside, Felipe took the lead. He went around the side of the building and headed for a trail through the wild area behind the Sanctuary. It led, I knew, to an old cemetery. Maida and Lucy followed Felipe, laughing and calling to him. I moved more slowly, enjoying both the sunshine and the chance to think.

Maida and Lucy had disappeared around a curve in the trail when I heard the sound of something moving through the underbrush on my right. I froze immediately, images of the creature we had spotted the night before playing in my head. At least, I told myself, it was daylight out this time, and I would be able to see what I was running away from.

There was more rustling, and I saw a flash of movement. I quickly laid a plan in my head: if I ran forward, I would risk getting Felipe and the girls into the chase. If I headed back toward the Sanctuary, I could lead the creature away from them, and I could get help.

I slowly pivoted until I was facing back the way I had come. Just as I was about to start running, I saw movement again, and I clearly caught a glimpse of a human leg.

"Who's there?" I called.

"Hang on!" It was Zach's voice, and in a few moments, he pushed his way between two tall, scrubby bushes.

"What are you doing?" I asked, relief flooding through me. "Also, welcome back to being a human."

"Being a wolf is more fun," Zach grumbled. "At least I got in a good run this morning before I changed back. And what I'm doing is collecting firewood. I like to pick up pieces from the ground so I don't have to chop down a living tree."

"And, in the meantime, scaring me half to death. I heard you and was convinced that creature from last night was stalking me."

"That werewolf," Zach said confidently. "It was definitely a werewolf. I could smell them when I went out after the Sanctuary closed last night, which is why I came back to round up you, Gunnar, and Malcolm. I didn't think it was safe to go after an unknown werewolf by myself."

"Do you have any idea who it might be?"

"Someone new in town. If another wolf had been in Nightmare for a while, I would know it by now. Unlike Malcolm, I do recognize the scent of my kind."

"And that someone is in human form again, like you, now that the moon is past its full. Who do we know of that's new in town?"

"Maybe there's something your ex hasn't told you about himself," Zach said, giving me a lopsided grin.

"I highly doubt he's supernatural. But, yes, Mark is new here. And there's Trent and his ex-wife, Stacy. But I've seen all three of them during the last three days, and not one of them had a tail."

Zach was nodding. "They were all human during the full moon, so it can't be one of them."

"Who have I not seen the past three days?" I mused. "If we're focusing on people associated with the stunt show, I haven't seen Darla, the costume designer, but she's not new in town, anyway."

"She could be newly turned into a werewolf," Zach suggested, "but that's highly unlikely."

I gasped. "There's someone else I haven't seen during the full moon, and she is new in town: the show's horse trainer, Laura!"

CHAPTER EIGHTEEN

"It makes sense!" I continued. "When I told Norman, the show manager, that I wanted to chat with Laura, he said she had taken the day off because she was so exhausted from keeping the horses calm during the investigation. That was Thursday, the first full day you were a wolf, too, Zach!"

"And I bet she was long gone before the sun set on Wednesday. It's not easy to hold down a job when you have to call in sick three days a month," Zach said sympathetically.

"I'm sure it isn't, but from what people have been saying, I understand Laura is very good at her job. Officer Reyes even said she has a way with animals."

"Because she is one!" Zach tilted his head back and laughed. I always found it a little spooky when he did that, because there was the hint of a howl in the sound. He quickly sobered, though. "If this Laura woman is a werewolf, then did she kill Billy with her claws?"

"That's something we have to find out."

"When you talk to her, let me come," Zach said earnestly. "This really is eerily similar to Jared Barker's murder, and I know what it's like to be your top suspect. It's hard enough to be new in town and a werewolf. Add accused of murder to the list, and she might get so worked up that she turns temporarily."

"I would appreciate your help. Plus, if she isn't a killer, she might be a good person for you to know. You'll have someone other than Felipe to run around with every month."

As if on cue, Felipe came careening around the corner just then. Something was clamped in his jaws, and as he got closer to me, I saw it was a bone. "Is he digging up bodies in the cemetery?" I yelped.

Zach leaned down and plucked the bone out of Felipe's mouth. "No, it's from a deer. Go get it, boy!" Zach threw the bone, and Felipe took off after it.

Lucy came around the corner next, shouting Felipe's name and giggling. "He just ran off!" she explained as she sailed past us.

Maida was next, moving much slower than Lucy. "I'm going to ask for light-up sneakers like she wears," she commented.

Zach returned to collecting wood while I followed the girls back to the Sanctuary. Felipe promptly curled up in a corner of the entryway and began to gnaw on the bone.

At Maida and Lucy's request, I called Nick and asked if it was okay for Lucy to spend the afternoon at the Sanctuary. He readily said yes, and the girls headed upstairs. As they went, I heard Maida say something about a spell book, and I hoped they wouldn't get themselves into too much magical trouble.

I went back to my apartment and caught up on laundry and dusting. Nick had agreed to pick Lucy up on his way home from the garage, so I had nowhere to be until work that night.

By the time I showed up at the Sanctuary for the second time that day, I was ready for some company and conversation. It had felt strangely lonely in my apartment, even though it was usually nice to have some solitude. Maybe I just needed a play date, too, I told myself.

I was happy when Justine assigned me to the front doors that evening, because I would definitely get my fill of talking to people as I tore tickets. And, when I had my break, I got the chance to chat with Mori, since she had her break at the same time.

Things were going well, and I was having one of those nights where I was aware of just how much I enjoyed my job and my co-workers. My happy little bubble burst, though, when I looked up to take the tickets of the next people in line and found myself staring into Mark's eyes.

"And here I thought I might get to see you in some ridiculous getup!" Mark grinned at me. "We thought since you came to our show, we should return the favor!"

I looked past Mark to find out who "we" included and saw Trent talking to a couple of women who looked like they were in their twenties. His smile was even flashier than Mark's, and I heard him say something about getting the women on the stunt show's guest list.

Mark held out two tickets, and as I tore them and handed the larger sections back to him, he said, "We had to pay to get in."

"Justine and I paid to see your show," I pointed out.

"We'll have to work out a trade deal if our show and your haunted house are going to have a relationship."

I wanted to gag at that comment, but I kept a straight look on my face as I told Mark and Trent to have a good time.

I hoped Theo and Seraphina would make them scream.

Mark and Trent had come through less than an hour before closing. That made sense, since Trent would have had to perform earlier in the evening, and he had probably showered and changed before coming to the Sanctuary.

Zach shut the ticket window at ten minutes before midnight, and soon, the last guests had gone past me, and I closed the front door. I always stashed my purse in one of the lockers inside the staff ladies' room, so I went there to retrieve it.

When I returned to the entryway, the first thing I saw was Gunnar's backside. His wings were extended, and he turned slightly, like he was showing them off. I caught a glimpse of Mark and Trent standing in front of him.

"It looks so real!" Mark said. "What an incredible costume!"

"Mark," I heard Damien say. He was just coming from the direction of his office. He pulled his mirrored sunglasses out of the inner pocket of his midnight-blue suit jacket and slid them on.

Uh-oh.

"Damien Shackleford, just the man I wanted to see!" Mark planted both hands on his hips. "What a great thing you've got going on here! Do you have a few minutes to chat?"

"Sure," Damien said tightly.

I couldn't tell if Mark was oblivious to the tension, or if he was willfully ignoring it. As Damien led the way to his office, he introduced Trent in a tone that implied Damien should be wowed to meet him.

I hadn't been invited to the impromptu meeting, but I tagged along, anyway. If there was a chance of Damien's emotions spiking, I wanted to be on hand to help as much as I could.

When we reached Damien's office, Mark and Trent settled into the two oxblood leather chairs in front of Damien's massive desk. That left me to stand behind them, which gave me a good vantage point to observe Damien, who slid into his chair, folded his hands on the desk, and prompted, "What would you like to chat about?"

"You've got an incredible thing going here," Mark said again, waving a hand regally. "A haunted house, and a historic building? I bet there are grants you could get from historic societies, maybe even the government, for restoration on a place like this."

"I'm sure it's something my father has already looked into."

"Your father?" Mark asked hesitantly.

"He owns the Sanctuary, not me."

Trent leaned toward Mark and said something too low for me to hear, but Mark nodded and said to Damien, "Yes, that's right. The man who went missing a while back. What a shame. All the more reason for you to spruce this place up. Keep it thriving in his memory."

Damien's fingers curled more tightly around themselves. "He's not dead."

"Of course not, of course not." Mark finally seemed to realize he was straying into sensitive territory, so he wisely changed the subject. "Your props and costumes are top-notch. That gargoyle of yours looks like he could really take flight!"

I had to cover my mouth to keep from giggling at that. *You have no idea*, I thought.

"Anyway, this little town of yours really draws in the tourists, and I think it's important for the local attractions to stick together." Mark leaned forward eagerly. "Maybe we can work out a combo ticket, so tourists can be thrilled by the stunt show, then come here to get scared! Perhaps we can set up a special Halloween edition of the show each October, and you can help us put it together."

"I thought you were Trent's manager," Damien said. "Are you working with Norman to run the show, too?"

Mark's head tilted slightly, and his shoulders twitched. It was something he did whenever he was stretching the truth. "Norman is open to my guidance. He knows the show needs a bit of a boost. So, what do you say? Should we discuss some opportunities?"

Damien stood. "If we do, I'd prefer to have Norman present. He's the one my father had a relationship with, and until I hear otherwise, he's still the manager of the show."

"Very well," Mark said, his disappointment obvious. "In the meantime, tell me, how is Olivia fitting in at your haunted house? This job isn't anything like what she was doing in Nashville."

"She's standing right behind you," Damien pointed out. "You can ask her yourself."

"I'm sure she'd say she's thriving here," Mark said. I couldn't see his smile, but I knew it was plastered in place. "I want the truth, so I'm asking you."

A bang echoed through the office, and I looked over to see a thick book open on the stone hearth. Mark leaped out of his chair, and his words came out in a rush. "She seems to be doing great, really. You know, it's awfully late, and Trent has two shows tomorrow, so we should get going."

Mark brushed past me with barely a nod. Trent, who seemed confused by Mark's hasty exit, looked at me apologetically as he followed. "Good night, Olivia. It was nice to see you again."

"Good night, gentlemen," I said. I shut the office door and turned to Damien with a snicker. "I think that book brought up some bad memories of flying brochures."

"He's got every right to be paranoid. How dare he talk about you like that? Right in front of you, no less." Damien pulled off his sunglasses and stared at the door like he wanted to charge through it.

Again, I had to wonder if Mark had always been like that. A little bit, I decided. It was like Mark's bad habits, which had been in the background before, had become his most prominent traits.

"At least you didn't hit him with the book," I commented as I stooped to pick it up. Like the last book Damien had thrown with his mind, this one had fallen open. Again, there was a bookmark between the pages.

Damien stepped up next to me and pressed his fingers against the folded piece of paper that had been inserted into the book. "Maybe the bookmarks are significant, somehow."

I was about to ask Damien if he was reading my mind when he continued, "My power might be pulling the books off the shelves, but what if I'm not the one choosing the books? Is my mother trying to give us a message by showing us the bookmarks?"

CHAPTER NINETEEN

"You think Lucille is using her psychic abilities to select what books come off the shelves and which pages fall open?" I watched as Damien picked up the bookmark. It looked like a handwritten letter.

"We know her presence is here, even if she's not quite what we'd call a ghost." Damien unfolded the letter and read, *"Dear Baxter, I got your note about the new costumes, and I can tell by your description they are extremely good quality. I'd be happy to come by next week to make the alterations to them, and I am especially excited about adding the feather details you've requested. It will be a welcome break from the wool and cotton I most often have in my hands. Tuesday morning works just fine for me. Yours, John Rainwater."*

I frowned. "It's a note from a tailor." Even as I spoke, I was already looking for the book Damien had mentally ripped from its shelf earlier. "Let's see if there's a connection between it and the first bookmark."

There wasn't. The first one had been the thank-you note from the firefighters, and we couldn't find anything to link the two bookmarks together. As we replaced the books on the shelf, I said, "You just need to keep getting upset, so this happens again, and we can look for a pattern."

"If Mark keeps popping up, that won't be a problem."

I gazed at Damien as I wondered, again, if he was jealous. There must have been something in my expression that told him what I was thinking, because his mouth twitched, and he looked away. That, in turn, made me feel embarrassed.

It was time to go.

"I'll see you tomorrow," I said. "Sorry you got ambushed by the dynamic duo tonight."

Damien gave me a soft smile. "For the record, you fit in great here. You were meant to come to the Sanctuary."

My embarrassment disappeared as I beamed at Damien. "I know."

Zach was just coming out of his office as I passed by it. "What's the plan?" he asked me.

I shrugged. "I guess we go ask Laura if she's a werewolf."

"Let's start with a friendly chat, shall we? We can get a feel for her, and if I can get a good sniff, we won't even have to ask her if she's a werewolf."

"Is that really how you do it? You're going to say hello, then lean in and smell her?"

"I promise to be more subtle than that."

Zach and I agreed to go to the show a little before one o'clock the following afternoon, so we could talk to Laura prior to the two o'clock performance. After that, I was finally able to get out the door and go home.

I was still asleep on Sunday morning when my phone rang, and I answered it groggily. I was surprised to hear Damien's voice on the other end, not because it was him calling me—my caller I.D. had informed me of that—but because of how excited he sounded.

"Can you come to the mine this morning? There's something I want to try."

I agreed, and twenty minutes later, I was heading out the door with a travel mug full of coffee. When I got to the mine, I was surprised to find the door wide open. I was worried someone had broken in, but Damien was calmly putting away dishes when I poked my head inside.

"Your door is open," I said. Talk about pointing out the obvious.

"It was a little stuffy in here." Damien dried his hands and pointed to a coffee maker on the kitchen counter. "There's more, too."

I yawned. "I'll probably need it. I assume you called me here to practice?"

"Yes. You calmed me down during lunch on Thursday. And that, in turn, dialed back the psychic reaction I was having to being upset."

"Right. I was totally focused on you being calm."

"What if you can do more than that?"

"I don't understand."

"You conjured my calm, but can you conjure control? If you focus hard enough on me controlling my power, maybe I can learn to guide what I do with my mind."

I nodded slowly. "You think I can do more than make your power go away."

"It's worth finding out, don't you think?"

"I'm ready when you are." I sat on the couch and took a sip of my coffee. "Let me know when you're upset enough that we can try."

I finished my coffee, refilled my mug, and was halfway through it when Damien sat down next to me with a sigh. "I can't do it." He had been pacing back and forth, and at one point, he had walked right out the open front door.

I patted his leg. "I never thought I'd know someone who was upset about not being able to get upset."

"I'm just too happy this morning. It's after eleven. How about we grab lunch? Maybe my order will come out wrong, and I'll get so mad I'll send plates sailing through the air like tiny flying saucers."

"The Lusty Lunch Counter is unlikely to get your order wrong, but yes, let's go eat."

I hadn't realized The Lusty was such a popular spot on Sundays, and when we arrived, there was nowhere to sit. We lingered around the entrance for about ten minutes before two spots at the counter opened up. By the time Damien and I had eaten, there was a line of people waiting to be seated.

We were nearly out the door before I spotted Darla. She was waiting in line with someone who was much younger but looked a lot like her. A son, probably.

"Hi, Darla. Nice shirt!" Maybe nice wasn't quite the right word, since it was almost as ostentatious as the one Trent had been wearing during his costume fitting. It was, however, eye-catching. The blue plaid Western shirt had brown leather patches on the shoulders and a line of short brown fringe down the arms. A small tag sewn onto the front pocket read *Wilder West* in an old-fashioned looking font.

Darla smoothed her shirt proudly. "Thank you! I'm wearing it in Billy's honor. This is a leftover from the Western wear line Billy had once wanted to run. Turns out, he was just a small-town dreamer, but I made some neat designs for him."

"Surely Billy wanted to get out of Nightmare and work one of the bigger shows," I said offhandedly. "I can't imagine he wanted to be a small-town guy his whole life."

"He did get out of Nightmare, for a while," Darla answered. She took a step toward me and lowered her voice. "He was a rising star at a theme park in California before Norman blackmailed him into coming back."

CHAPTER TWENTY

My mouth was moving, but nothing was coming out. I was too stunned to respond.

Darla's eyes lit up, and her shoulders shook with laugher. She was loving my reaction to her news.

"But I thought Norman and Billy were friends?" I finally said.

"Of course they were. Right up until Billy's death. This all happened years ago."

"The blackmailing happened years ago?"

"And the embezzling."

Darla looked even more amused as my mouth fell open. "That's right," she said, nodding slowly. "Billy joined the show at the theme park, and he planned to never come back to Nightmare. About six months after he left, though, Norman was going through the show's finances, and there was money missing from the year before. He did some digging and realized Billy had been the one who stole it. The show's popularity was flagging without Billy as the star, so Norman blackmailed him. He said he'd take the matter to the authorities if Billy didn't come back. Billy rightly decided living in Nightmare was a lot better than sitting in jail."

"Wow." It was all I could get out. My brain was too

busy thinking that Norman had a growing list of motives for killing Billy.

Darla gave my arm a nudge. "Of course, this was all a long time ago. Water under the bridge."

Maybe not.

I thanked Darla for the information, and Damien and I headed out. When I told him I was picking Zach up shortly before one so we could go talk to Laura, Damien insisted on coming along. He added that we would likely run into Mark at the show, which would give us a chance to test out Damien's new theory about how our abilities might be able to work in tandem. So, instead of taking me back to my car, which was parked at the mine, Damien headed straight for the Sanctuary.

When Zach came outside, he didn't seem at all surprised to see Damien's car instead of mine. I got out of the passenger seat so I could squeeze into the back. I was shorter than Zach, so it was a lot easier for me to wedge myself into the tiny space. Before I could get back in the car, though, Zach whispered in my ear, "I see you brought your boyfriend."

"You don't quit, do you?" I asked.

"Quit what?" Damien called from the driver's seat.

"Nothing," Zach and I answered in unison as I flashed him my best *See what you did?* look.

I had been so preoccupied by Mark's unexpected visit to the Sanctuary that I had completely forgotten to tell Damien about our suspicion that Laura was a werewolf. So, as we drove, Zach and I filled him in. I ended with, "And Zach says we can't just ask her if she's a wolf when the moon is full."

"I think that's good advice," Damien said. We had reached the stunt show by then, and he pulled into a parking space. "And, Olivia, I recommend that you try to conjure her cooperation."

Laura staying calm and opening up to us was what I kept in mind as we went in search of her. We found her in the barn, prepping the horses for the show. As we approached, she slung a saddle over the back of a tall horse like it was the lightest thing in the world. I knew Zach was really strong, but I had never before considered that it was a trait of his kind.

"Hi, Laura," I called.

She looked up and brushed a few stray locks of hair out of her face. "Oh, hi. You're back." Laura looked at Damien and Zach, who were standing on either side of me, with outright curiosity. I realized that with the way they were standing, they looked like my bodyguards.

"Damien is my boss, and Zach is a co-worker," I clarified. Then, remembering Laura was new in Nightmare, I added, "At Nightmare Sanctuary Haunted House. It's over on the north end of town."

"Yeah, I know. The rumor around town is that the witches there aren't just playing a part." Laura said it in a way that implied she believed the rumor.

"Who knows?" I said mysteriously. "Norman told us you were exhausted after keeping the horses calm in the wake of Billy's murder. Are you feeling better?"

Laura nodded emphatically. "Much better. It took me three days to recover, but I'm back at it."

Three days? Oh, yeah, this is our wolf. She has to be.

"It was a beautiful full moon this last time around," Zach said. "Don't you think?"

Laura picked up a brush and began to run it along the neck of the horse she had just saddled. "Very pretty."

"I like going for a run at night when it's that bright," Zach continued. "It feels magical."

"I'm sure."

I appreciated Zach's efforts, but Laura was clearly not going to fall for his werewolf-related comments. Besides, I had more important things on my mind, like why Laura might have killed Billy in the first place. Sure, it looked like she might have clawed him up, but why? I wasn't aware that she had any kind of motive.

"It's got to be weird carrying on the show without Billy," I said.

For a moment, I didn't think Laura was going to respond, but eventually, she said, "It's not too weird for me, because I'm so new. I only worked with him for a few weeks."

"Ah, so you don't have all the stories the others do about what a pain he could be."

Laura stopped brushing and turned to me with wide eyes. "I have stories, all right. Billy started giving me a hard time on day one, saying I didn't know the right way to care for the horses. He even accused me of training them to not like him!"

"How could he think that?" Zach asked.

"I had a chat with the show's former trainer, and it sounds like he went through the same thing," I told Laura.

"Yeah, he and I have been hanging out, and we spend a lot of our time swapping stories about Billy. I don't know what we're going to bond over now!"

"You know Leo?" I asked, surprised. "I would have thought he'd hold a grudge against you since you took his old job."

Laura cocked her head. "No, he's a good guy, and he knows I'm not the reason he lost his job. Billy made things hard, for me and for Leo. Neither one of us is at fault for that." She turned and began to brush the horse again, and I heard her mutter, "He understands."

I wanted to ask what, exactly, Leo understood. Were she and Leo both involved in Billy's murder?

Before I could ask, though, Laura said, "I need to get

the horses ready and move them over to the arena. Did you need anything from me?"

"We just wanted to say hi," Zach said. "I'm a big fan of animals, and I think it's great that you get to work with horses for a living."

Laura flashed a wide smile at Zach. "I'm so lucky. I love these creatures."

"Nice meeting you, Laura," Damien said.

I said goodbye, and we turned to leave as Laura led the horse toward a door at the far end of the barn.

"Well?" I prompted Zach as soon as we were outside. We had taken a different door out of the barn, and we found ourselves inside the corral.

"There could have been twenty werewolves in there, and I wouldn't have been able to sniff out a single one of them. The smell of the horses was too strong."

"But she has to be our werewolf, right?"

"She did say she was out for three days," Damien pointed out.

Zach looked over his shoulder wistfully. "I wish we'd had more time to talk to her. She's so pretty, and I would love to hear her stories about training horses."

"Oh, Zach," I cooed, "do you have a girlfriend?"

Zach looked like he was about to retort, but he gave me an appreciative nod, instead. "I deserved that."

We hadn't learned whether Laura was a werewolf, but we had gotten some very valuable information out of her. I started counting on my fingers. "Norman, Leo, and Laura all seem to get along with each other, and they all had at least one reason to want Billy dead. Are we looking at a team effort here?"

"You said the show would allegedly get money from Billy's estate," Damien said. "Leo might have wanted revenge, but for Norman and Laura, they'd be saving the show and their jobs with an influx of cash."

"I think we have to consider other suspects," Zach said.

I was about to tease him about having a crush on a possible murderer, but the words died on my lips as I looked where Zach was pointing.

Stacy Nash was standing inside the corral, running her fingers over deep claw marks in the side of the barn.

CHAPTER TWENTY-ONE

"That's Stacy Nash, Trent's ex-wife," I said. "But we know she's not a werewolf. I saw her during the full moon, remember?"

"You just said this could be a team effort," Damien reminded me. "Maybe she isn't the one who clawed Billy to pieces, but that doesn't mean she isn't involved."

Stacy was still staring at the side of the barn, so she didn't realize she had an audience. "You two stay here," I said. "I'm going to have a little chat with her, ex to ex."

As I got closer to Stacy, I called, "We meet again!" She whirled around with a startled look on her face, then relaxed a bit when she recognized me.

"What do you think did this?" Stacy asked, putting her fingers against the claw marks again.

I couldn't very well say it had probably been a werewolf. "The police think it might have been a coyote."

"Do you think the animal that made these marks is the same animal that killed Billy?" Stacy looked around wildly, as if she expected to see a coyote loping through the corral toward us that very moment.

"Possibly."

"What if it comes after Trent, too?"

I'd been having mixed feelings about Stacy, but with that question, she stopped straddling the line between suspicious and sympathetic. She had claimed she followed Trent to Nightmare just to make sure she got the money he owed her, but her tone and the horrified look on her face told a different story. She still cared about him. A lot.

Of course, I argued with myself, *if she still loves him, maybe she did commit murder. It just wasn't for the reason I thought it was.*

"Billy was very good at making people dislike him," I said carefully. "As long as Trent is being kind and not engaging in anything underhanded, I think he's safe."

"What does a wild animal care about kindness?" Stacy asked.

"What I mean is, if someone let a wild animal into the corral, then they did it because they wanted to hurt or kill Billy. If there's no one who wants to hurt or kill Trent, then you don't have a thing to worry about."

I had thought I was reassuring Stacy, but her face paled. "He made a few people mad in Nashville."

I sighed. "Let's hope they didn't follow him here, like you did. Are you catching the show today?"

"Yeah," Stacy said vaguely.

I assumed her mind was busy making a list of people who had a reason to set a wild animal on Trent. I walked with her toward the gate in the corral fence, and as we reached it, Darla walked past with an armful of dark denim fabric.

"Hello, ladies," Darla said as she stopped and nodded at us. "You picked a gorgeous day to come to the show!"

"It is beautiful," I agreed. It was nearly December, but the sun was out, and I was warm enough in jeans and a lightweight cream-colored sweater.

"Darla, I'm so glad you found the fabric you were looking for! Trent will look great in this." Stacy reached over the fence and ran her fingers along the denim.

"You two know each other?" I asked, surprised.

"We met a few days ago," Darla clarified.

"Hey, Stacy!" It was Laura, who was walking past with a horse in tow.

Before I could ask, Stacy gave a short laugh and said, "Yes, I know Laura, too. I've met everyone on staff here, and they all seem like great people. Plus, Laura is as interested in Trent making money as I am. If he's successful, then so am I, and so is everyone involved with the show. We all need this to work."

I was creating an elaborate "everyone is in on it" theory when Darla's voice broke into my thoughts. "What did you do to your cardigan?"

Stacy reached down and touched a long rip in her sky-blue cardigan. "Oh, I caught it on a rusty nail in the barn."

"I bet we can save it. Let's go take a look."

"See you, Olivia." Stacy gave me a wave, looking like her fear for Trent had passed, at least for the time being. As she let herself out of the gate, I heard her say to Darla, "I've always wanted to learn to knit. If I stick around here for a while, can you teach me?"

I wonder if Trent knows his ex is thinking about staying in Nightmare.

Once Darla and Stacy were out of earshot, I called Zach over and pointed toward the side of the barn. "Can you tell if those claw marks are from a werewolf?"

"The marks are deep," Zach said. "I took a closer look while you were chatting with the blonde. I can't tell you they definitely came from a werewolf, but I can tell you that not a lot of creatures can make gouge marks like that."

Damien came strolling up to us, even though he was looking in the direction Darla and Stacy had gone. "Did you ladies have a nice chat?"

"She seems more scared than suspicious," I admitted.

"Maybe she was an actor in Nashville," Zach said.

"I think it's more likely she's not over Trent yet, and she's genuinely worried about him." I tilted my head left and right, feeling like my neck muscles were tightening up. I chalked it up to tension from the past week. "Everyone I talk to seems to have a motive."

"I wondered if that's why you came to my house the other day." Leo Whitehall appeared at my side, a lopsided smile on his face. "Though you did come up with a nice excuse for the visit."

I felt heat in my cheeks. "You got me," I admitted.

"I've had two gorgeous women visit me in the past week. I'm not going to nitpick over the reasons you both stopped in."

"What are you doing here?" I asked in as casual a tone as I could. "I figured you wouldn't want to risk running into Norman."

"I came to see if the new guy is any good," Leo said. He gave me an exaggerated wink. "One of the employees will let me in the back gate of the arena, because there's no way I'm giving Norman any of my money. Now, if you'll excuse me, I want to say hi to Laura before I go find a seat."

Leo moved in the direction of the barn, but I pointed toward the arena. "She's taking horses over since the show starts soon."

Leo pivoted and headed along the path to the arena, and I looked at my companions. "Do we want to catch the show, too? Unlike Leo, we'll have to buy tickets."

Damien made a grumpy sound. "I figured Mark would be happy to hook us up with tickets."

"He would, but I wouldn't be happy to accept them."

Zach shrugged. "I don't feel the need to see a fancy cowboy ride a horse."

Damien nodded in agreement.

We made it as far as the corral gate, because Norman

was walking right toward us. Leo's timing had been good. If he had lingered another minute with us, he would have come face-to-face with the guy who had fired him.

I was feeling frustrated by the long list of suspects and motives, because we still had no clear indication of who had murdered Billy. That was the only excuse I could think of for why I was so blunt with Norman. I didn't even say hello to him before I blurted, "Is it true Billy embezzled from the show?"

Norman's face had lit up when he recognized Damien and me, and when I asked my question, his face froze like that for a few seconds. Slowly, his eyebrows drew down. "Where did you hear that? No, don't tell me. It doesn't matter. Yes, I once caught Billy embezzling."

If Norman had been shocked by my directness, then I was equally shocked by his. I hadn't expected him to own up to the truth so quickly, because he must have known it made him look suspicious.

Norman and I stared at each other briefly before I said, "Here's what I don't get. If Billy had family money, then why did he feel the need to steal from the show?"

Norman's portly belly bounced as he laughed. "He used to have family money. He spent it years ago."

"All of it?" I asked.

"Every penny. Once it was gone, the salary he was getting from me apparently wasn't enough, so he started skimming cash from the ticket office. Then, he up and went to California, probably hoping he'd never get caught."

"But you went back and did a thorough audit," I prompted.

Norman nodded. "Things just weren't adding up. We were packing the house back in those days, for every show, but our accounting kept coming up short."

I realized Norman could have killed Billy to get

revenge, but as Darla and Norman had both mentioned, the embezzling had happened years before. It would have been strange for Norman to wait so long to exact his revenge. I had thought it was more likely Norman had killed Billy so he could get his hands on the family money.

But, as it turned out, there was no family money. There hadn't been for years, and Norman had known it.

Norman turned to Damien and started chatting with him while I thought about what that meant. For one thing, it meant Norman was very likely not the killer. For another, it meant Leo had either been wrong about Billy leaving money to the show, or he had lied to put Norman in the spotlight.

CHAPTER TWENTY-TWO

"Come on," I heard Norman say to Damien and Zach. "You haven't seen the show unless you've seen it from my box!"

That finally pulled me out of my head and into the present moment. Zach gave me a wry look and said, "I guess we're going to see the show, after all."

Damien had clearly shifted into what I thought of as a Chamber of Commerce demeanor: polite, friendly, and maybe a tad too enthusiastic. "That would be great," he said to Norman. "I haven't seen the show since I was a kid."

"It's better than ever! This new stunt rider, Trent, he's as authentic as they come! So much talent and star power. Let me tell you, this kid is going to make our show the talk of the town!" Norman continued talking in exclamation points as he led the way toward the arena. Damien kept pace with him, inserting *"mm-hmm"* and *"for sure"* at just the right moments.

Zach and I trailed behind, and he seemed as lost in his own thoughts as I was. I knew what it was like to have plenty of money, and, like Billy, I knew how scary it seemed when it was all gone. I felt my resentment toward Mark rise, and I pressed a hand to my heart. *Remember what*

Mama said about him, I reminded myself. He might have squandered our money and thrown my life into upheaval, but he needed compassion.

I would never say it was easy to feel that way toward him, but I was trying my best.

Norman's box was a private suite built above the bench seating on one side of the arena. There were chairs at the front and a bar at the back. All of us declined his offer of a beer, but I gladly accepted a diet soda.

We chatted with Norman until the show began, then we fell silent. The opening routine was vastly different from the one I had seen when I had been there with Justine.

It was also vastly better.

"Wow," I said. "Norman, this opener is stunning!"

"Isn't it?" Norman looked like a proud father. "Trent and Laura have been working really hard, and so have the other riders in the show. The choreography is just thrilling. Listen to the crowd!"

"They love it," Damien said. He sounded genuinely impressed.

Trent had ridden out wearing a dark-brown duster cinched tight around his body and a matching cowboy hat pulled down nearly to his eyebrows. About ten minutes into the show, he threw the hat into the air, then deftly slipped out of the duster and tossed it to the ground, revealing an outfit so ridiculous I had to clap a hand over my mouth to keep myself from laughing.

The shirt was red with white fringe across the chest and down the arms. The cuffs were white, too, and they had a band of rhinestones around them. Every time Trent moved, light flashed from his wrists. Trent's pants had probably started life as plain-old blue jeans, but Darla had added white fringe down the legs. Instead of stopping there, she had added a row of rhinestones on each side of the fringe. We were too far away to see the rhinestones themselves, but judging by the way Trent's legs were sparkling, I knew that was what they were.

I felt a hand on mine. Damien was sitting next to me, and he was biting his lower lip. He inhaled deeply and squeezed my fingers.

We aren't going to laugh. We aren't going to laugh. We aren't going to laugh.

It was the most ridiculous thing I had tried to conjure yet, but I knew Damien and I needed all the help we could get. I glanced at Zach, and he was staring open-mouthed at Trent.

Thankfully, Norman seemed to take our silence for awe. "Magnificent, isn't it? Kids all over town are going to want that same outfit!"

"Olivia, is that what cowboys in Nashville wear?" Damien asked me.

I had to take a couple of breaths before I could answer. "I've seen a few like that at the Grand Ole Opry, but Trent takes the cake."

"Cake with fringe on top," Zach muttered.

We aren't going to laugh.

As the show moved on and I got used to the glare from Trent's outfit, I was able to relax. The show was better than what I had seen the first time around, since the stunt riders had been able to get in more practice time with the new choreography. Plus, there had been additional changes that were definite improvements.

I didn't much care for Trent—he was a little too full of himself for my taste—but I could see why Norman was excited to have him as the star of the show. He was an incredibly talented stunt rider, and he had charisma that carried all the way up to the box where we sat.

When the show was over, Norman looked at the rest of us. "What did you think? Spectacular, isn't he?"

"You have every right to be excited about the future of the show," Damien said. "People are still cheering!"

That seemed to satisfy Norman, and he led the way out of the box and down to the arena's exit. He immediately started shaking hands with people and asking them if they had enjoyed themselves. When Norman stopped to shake a woman's hand, her son said, "I want a shirt like that!"

Wow. Norman was right.

We said goodbye, but Norman was so busy collecting accolades he barely noticed our departure. As we moved toward the parking lot, I overheard two men who looked to be in their thirties.

"I wonder where I can buy one," the first said.

"Check Nightmare Western Wear out on Mesquite Road," said the other. "I've seen a few fringed shirts there before."

"Yeah, but nothing like that!"

There was just no accounting for taste.

Damien drove us back to the Sanctuary, where I hopped into my car and made the short drive back to the motel. I would only have a couple of hours at home before I needed to return for work that night, and the first order of business was a shower, followed by a quick nap.

With those things out of the way, I headed to the motel office to fill Mama in on the latest. She laughed when I told her about Trent's sparkly cowboy outfit. "Sounds to me like he's anxious to make his mark," she commented. "He wants people to forget Billy was ever there."

"He's doing a good job of it," I agreed, even as I wondered how much influence Mark might have had in the changes to the show. Trent's ridiculous outfit seemed like the embodiment of Mark and his newfound ambition.

"I had to conjure during the stunt show," I added. "Damien and I were trying so hard not to laugh at Trent's outfit that it took magic to keep us quiet."

"And you were successful?" Mama asked.

"I'm proud to say we did not lose our cool, even in the glare of a thousand rhinestones!"

"Tell me how it works." Mama was behind the counter, and she rested both hands on the edge and leaned forward eagerly. "How do you get into the minds of others?"

"I usually don't," I said thoughtfully. "I've made some things happen, but I haven't been able to control another person's thoughts or feelings. Except for Damien."

"And you just think about how you want him to feel?"

"Yes, but it's focused thinking. Single-minded. I've only done it while maintaining physical contact, so maybe that's a part of it."

Mama waggled her eyebrows. "Physical contact, huh?"

"Not like that!" I could feel myself blushing for the second time that day. "We just hold hands."

"Aww. That's so sweet." Mama's tone was teasing, but she also seemed pleased by my admission.

"Okay, I'm going back to my apartment now," I said in mock exasperation. "I'll see you later."

"Bye!" Mama drew out the word. "Let me know when you try conjuring via kissing!"

"It's not like that!" I said as I walked out the door. I was giggling so much, though, that it was impossible to sound truly offended.

Even though Mama had been teasing me, her comments got me thinking about Damien and how my conjuring worked with his psychic abilities. Did we have to maintain physical contact, or was my intention and mental focus enough to help him control his magic?

And, as Damien had mentioned, what else could I help him achieve? How much were we capable of together?

"You can bring him home."

I was only halfway back to my apartment, but I stopped walking as I heard the quiet whisper. I felt like the wind had just been knocked out of me. We were going to find Baxter. I knew it in that moment, because Lucille's spirit had just whispered it into my ear.

CHAPTER TWENTY-THREE

I didn't know why I was so certain it was Lucille's voice I had heard. I just knew it was. I wasn't scared or excited. Instead, I felt calm, like disembodied voices spoke to me all the time. Damien had once heard her voice on the wind while he was practicing in the middle of the desert, and Lucille had spoken to Mama in a dream. Lucille had been talking to Tanner and McCrory, too.

Damien had been a toddler when his mother disappeared, and no one had gotten any proof of her existence for four decades. Why, then, was she suddenly talking to so many of us? It was like she had woken up, and she was eager to help us find her husband.

"Thank you, Lucille," I whispered to the air. I turned and ran back to the motel office. When I burst through the door, the bell tinkled wildly, and Mama stood up from her desk, looking worried.

"It's okay!" I said, and it was only then I realized there were tears in my eyes. "She just spoke to me. I heard her!"

Mama didn't have to ask who I meant. She hustled around the counter and swept me up in a tight hug. "Oh, you lucky thing! What did my sister say to you?"

I told Mama the words I'd heard, adding, "I think she was reading my mind, because what she said was in answer to a question I was asking myself."

"You never know when a psychic is listening in," Mama quipped. She released me and stepped back, her eyes scanning the air around me. "Lucille, if you're still here, I miss you. Thank you for keeping an eye on Olivia."

Mama and I both cried and laughed. She was overjoyed that Lucille had spoken to me, and she was relieved to feel like it was only a matter of time before Baxter was found and brought home.

Eventually, though, I had to go get ready for work. I walked to my apartment slowly, listening for another whisper, but I didn't hear anything.

I left early for work so I could tell Damien I'd heard his mother, but his car wasn't even in the parking lot. Disappointed, I continued on to the dining room. My mood lifted as soon as I walked in and saw Mori and Malcolm huddled together in one corner. Felipe was running around them with another bone clamped in his jaws.

"You two look like you're hatching a plan," I said as I walked up to them.

"Have you read today's paper?" Malcolm asked.

I shook my head. Often, I would peruse *The Nightmare Journal* while I was in the motel office, but I hadn't looked at that day's edition.

Malcolm seemed pleased with my answer, because he stood up straighter, adjusted the lapels of his long black coat, and struck a pose that made him look like an actor about to give a monologue. "There's a story about Billy's murder, and you might find the details helpful in your investigation. Werewolf claws can cut deep, but not as deep as the additional wounds discovered during the autopsy."

"Additional wounds?" I asked.

Mori lifted her chin. "After reading the article, I asked Zach how deep his claws can go. He said around three inches. The wounds they found on Billy were up to six inches long."

"Where were they on his body?"

"The article doesn't specify," Malcolm answered, "but the speculation is that those wounds are what dealt the fatal blow to the star of the stunt show."

"So dramatic," I said, shaking my head. I held a hand against my ribcage. "Six inches is deep. That could do a lot of damage."

"Deep but narrow, according to the article," Mori pointed out.

"Like a screwdriver, or a rusty old barn nail," I mused. "What if the claw marks were meant to cover up the real cause of death? The killer might have hoped the police would call it an animal attack and not even bother with an autopsy."

"That's our assumption, as well," Malcolm said. "So, if the claw marks were a cover-up, did Laura make them while she was in werewolf form? Assuming, of course, she is our mysterious werewolf."

"And if she did make them," I added, "was it because she also caused the other wounds, or was she working with someone?"

Mori raised a finger. "We also have to consider she was coerced."

"Stranger and stranger. I wish we could just walk up to her and tell her we know her secret. We could answer a lot of questions if we could go straight to the source." After all, I figured, I had been straightforward with Norman earlier in the day, and it had yielded some valuable information about Billy's finances.

Felipe spit the bone onto the floor and rumbled softly.

"He agrees with me," I said, leaning down to give him a scratch under the chin.

"Asking point-blank is easier said than done," Mori

cautioned. "We don't want to put a murderer on her guard, if Laura is the guilty party."

"True. Maybe, until we figure out how to have that conversation with Laura, we can look into Billy's finances." I quickly explained what I had learned from Norman. "If we know how Billy lost his money, it might point us in a productive direction," I concluded.

"Talk to some of the old-timers," Mori advised. "There are plenty of gossip queens—"

"And kings!" Malcolm interjected.

"Yes. Gossipy busybodies are prolific in Nightmare. Start with your friend who works at the diner."

"Ella? She's in her twenties. Hardly an old-timer!" I said.

"But she'll know who comes in with all the scoop." Mori nodded confidently. "She can point you in the right direction."

"Good idea."

The dining room had been filling up as we talked, and it was soon time for us to take our seats for the family meeting. Justine assigned me to the haunted hospital vignette. It required me to put on a long, lank black wig that hung down in front of my face and a hospital gown that looked like it was spattered with blood. It wasn't nearly as glamorous as my pirate costume.

If Trent wore it, he'd add rhinestones.

After the meeting, I ran to Damien's office before changing into my costume, but he still wasn't there. "Where are you?" I said to the locked door. "Ugh!"

I channeled my frustration about not being able to talk to Damien into my makeup for the night. I aggressively applied pale foundation, dark circles under my eyes, and even some green tint around my lips. By the time I was done, I looked downright horrifying. I was definitely going to frighten people throughout the evening, and I wished

Theo was in the same vignette so we could have our competition. I knew I would win easily.

As it turned out, pretending to be a hospital patient infected with a monstrous virus was exactly what I needed. Once we opened for the night, the time sped past. I was surprised when Clara tapped me on the shoulder and told me it was time for my break. She had donned a long wig and a ratty hospital gown, too. Since she was relieving many of us throughout the night as it was time for our breaks, she had to swap costumes regularly. Clara didn't have the gruesome makeup on, but what she lacked in creepy looks she made up for with her acting. Even as I was disappearing through a door that led to the network of walkways behind the scenes, I heard a group of teenagers scream.

The rest of the night went just as quickly, and before I knew it, the overhead lights were on, and I was done for the evening. I practically ran to the costume room and changed back into my jeans and Sanctuary T-shirt, and then I headed for the bathroom to scrub the costume makeup off my face.

My face was clean, but I was self-conscious about not having any of my normal, everyday makeup on. It had been about a decade since I had loved my looks enough to go out with nothing but moisturizer on, and I felt like it was one of the most annoying things about being middle-aged. Leaving home without first applying at least foundation and a bit of eyebrow pencil was absolutely out of the question.

Still, I had to be satisfied with a face that didn't look dead and rotting, so I headed for Damien's office. The third time was the charm, because the door was open, and he was seated at his desk.

Damien looked up as I walked in. "You look nice," he said.

I glanced down at my outfit. "I look the same as I always do."

"I mean your face. You look...fresh. Kind of glowing."

I self-consciously pressed the fingers of one hand to my cheek. *I do?* "Thank you."

Damien's attention suddenly shifted, his eyes looking past me at the same time I heard footsteps. It was Zach, who was carrying a box wrapped with dark-green paper and topped with a gold bow.

"I meant to bring this by earlier," Zach said to Damien. "It was sitting in front of the door when I opened the ticket window tonight, and it's got your name on it."

Zach plunked the gift down onto Damien's desk. As he passed me on his way out, he said, "Tell me later what's in it, okay?"

I was curious, too. I watched as Damien lifted a small envelope tucked under the bow. He slid the card halfway out, and suddenly, I began to hear a humming noise. It seemed to be coming from all around me. I turned a circle as I looked for the source of the sound, and I quickly realized it appeared to be coming from everywhere because every single thing in the office was vibrating. The decor on the fireplace mantel, the items on Damien's desk, even the chairs were buzzing like an electrical current was running through them.

"Damien?" I wasn't sure if I should lurch forward and grab his hand to conjure control for him, or if I should duck and cover.

"It's from Mark." Damien spoke quietly. "The card says it's a little present for his new friend."

I spared a brief moment to feel annoyed at Mark, then quickly returned my attention to Damien. I stepped forward, my hand held out toward him. "I have good news to share with you. Why don't you wait to open that until after I've told you? Otherwise, I'm afraid you'll pull every single book off the shelves."

It was only then that Damien seemed to realize what was happening. His gaze slowly traveled around the room. "Oh." Without another word, he leaned across his desk and took my hand.

I closed my eyes and focused on Damien being calm. *What I want more than anything else,* I thought fervently, *is for Damien to calm down.*

The sound of every single thing in the office vibrating with energy began to quiet, but it must have been at least three minutes before there was total silence. I cracked one eye open and looked at Damien, who had also closed his eyes. I pulled my hand back and said, "We're definitely making progress on the control aspect. Now we just need to work on the guiding your power part."

Damien opened his eyes and rapped his knuckles against the top of the present. "We could work on me throwing this in the trash can with my mind."

"I'd be happy to help with that."

"Except now I'm too calm, thanks to you. But, like you said, we're making progress and learning things. This helps us know how to structure our practice sessions."

"Practice? Are you two starting your own show?"

I whirled around and saw Trent Nash standing in the doorway. He was looking downright plain, wearing jeans without a single rhinestone or length of fringe, and he had swapped his usual Western shirts for a plain gray sweatshirt.

Zach was right on Trent's heels. "Sorry!" he called over Trent's shoulder. "I tried to stop him."

"Is it just you?" Damien asked Trent.

When Trent nodded, Damien waved him inside. "It's fine, Zach. Trent's welcome in my office anytime." Damien didn't have to add that he was being so agreeable only because Trent didn't have Mark in tow.

"I sure appreciate it," Trent said, his smile wide.

Zach left, saying he was heading to Under the Undertaker's, and Trent quietly shut the door behind him. Once it was just the three of us standing there, Trent's expression turned sober.

"I'm glad you're here, too, Olivia," Trent said. He stepped forward and braced himself against the back of a chair. "I have some concerns about your ex-husband."

CHAPTER TWENTY-FOUR

"Who doesn't?" I asked sarcastically.

Damien, on the other hand, seemed to be taking Trent's statement a little more seriously. "You didn't know Olivia would be here with me, so you were prepared to talk to me privately. Why are you coming to me with these concerns?"

Trent took a deep breath, glanced behind him as if to make sure the door was still closed, then said quietly, "I don't know who I can trust at the show."

"Because you think one of your co-workers killed Billy?" I asked.

Trent seemed startled by the mere suggestion. "What? No. That is, I've considered one of them might be guilty, but that's not what brought me here tonight. I overheard Mark on the phone, and he said something about making a deal to the person on the other end."

I shook my head. "Why is that a concern? It seems like his normal behavior."

"Because I also heard him say he could use me as leverage. What does that even mean?"

Damien and I both shrugged, and Trent continued. "Look, Olivia, I don't want to speak ill of Mark. He got my career back on track. I know I talk a big game about my work in Nashville, but the truth is, I, uh, didn't leave the show there on good terms. Mark put this deal together for me. He found this job, he talked me up to Norman, and he's given me a real good new start. At the same time, I know he's a bit of a hustler. I don't want my career to be in jeopardy because he's off making side deals that involve me without my consent."

"So, what, you came here tonight to ask me if I'd give you career advice?" Damien asked.

"I want to know how I should handle the situation." Trent looked at me. "And, since you're here, I want to know if I can trust Mark."

"Just ask him what he was talking about," I said. "Tell him you overheard the conversation, and insist that you should be informed of any potential deals that involve you." *Poor Trent,* I thought. He was good-looking and a great showman, but he didn't have a lot of business savvy. Damien had nailed it: Trent had come to him hoping for career advice.

"Olivia is right," Damien said. "But I'd like to get back to what you said before. Tell us, why don't you trust your co-workers?"

Trent moved to the front of the chair and sank down into it. "They're all under his spell. They think Mark walks on water because he brought them their new star."

Damien and I exchanged a glance over Trent's head. "That's a compliment to you," I pointed out.

"I guess. But, if I try to raise concerns about Mark with the show staff, I know they'll tell me I'm being silly." Trent sat up and twisted around in his seat so he could look at me. "Will you talk to him, too? Please?"

Again, Damien and I looked at each other. It would be an awkward conversation to have, but at the same time, maybe Damien and I could turn the moment into a practice exercise. I knew Damien was thinking the same thing when he gave me a barely-perceptible nod.

"Okay," I conceded. "I'll have a chat with him. Damien and I will visit the show tomorrow."

"Thanks!" Trent's smile wasn't his big, crowd-pleasing one. Instead, he looked more like a child who'd been told they wouldn't be grounded, after all. Trent popped up from the chair with renewed energy. "I'll see you two tomorrow, then!" Soon, he was gone, and Damien and I were left shaking our heads at each other.

"Pick you up around noon?" Damien asked.

"Yeah. It will be good practice, and maybe we'll get to chat with Laura some more. In the meantime, I'm heading home. I need as much rest as possible before whatever tomorrow brings."

It was only after I got home that I realized I had forgotten to tell Damien my news about Lucille. Trent's arrival had pushed it right out of my mind.

Damien picked me up at noon on the dot on Monday, and as we drove to the stunt show, we agreed to take the same approach with Mark as we had with Laura. We were just going to have a nice, friendly chat. As soon as that was settled, I opened my mouth to relay my encounter with Lucille, but Damien's phone buzzed at the same time. He answered it on speaker phone, and I had to spend the rest of the drive listening to him discuss an order for fake spiderwebs.

Once we arrived at the stunt show, my determination to be sweet and casual nearly flew out the window when I caught sight of Mark near the corral. He was on his cell phone, as usual, but it was what he was wearing that threw me for a loop. His plaid Western shirt was yellow and blue, but the yellow was so bright Mark could have been used as a lighthouse beacon. The fringe was the same shade.

"Glad I brought my sunglasses," Damien said quietly as we walked forward.

Mark noticed us thirty seconds after we had stopped near him, and he held up one finger as he continued talking into his phone. Laura passed by us with three different horses in the time it took for him to finally wrap up the call.

"Thanks for waiting," Mark said as he hung up. "What brings you back here so soon?"

"It occurred to me that I know very little about your life here in Nightmare," I began. "Where are you staying?"

"At the Nightmare Grand."

Of course Mark had chosen the most expensive hotel in town. I couldn't imagine what his extended stay there was costing him—or whoever he had borrowed money from. I suspected the latter was more likely.

"You know there's a great diner just a few blocks from there," I said.

"We should grab dinner there tonight!" Mark tilted his head and smiled in a way that he knew made the dimple on his right cheek show.

I felt Damien stiffen beside me.

"I have plans," I said smoothly. "But I did want to ask if you need any help getting settled in. For instance, I know a great real estate agent."

A shovel propped against the corral fence suddenly fell over. *Did Damien just do that?*

"I'll need a good agent. I have no idea where to find a decent place in this town." Mark looked at Damien. "I hear you live in an old mine. Is that true?"

"My father converted it into a home."

"A home made of rock? With no windows?" Mark gave a little sniff. "I'm surprised you don't live at that old building the haunted house is in. Of course, it's probably a bit dank and dirty."

A bridle hanging from a hook on the side of the barn didn't fall off. It flew off, landing about ten feet away.

"The Sanctuary has been nicely restored," I said, somewhat sternly. "Many of the employees live in apartments upstairs, and they're very cozy spaces."

I heard a frustrated grunt and saw Laura standing at the door of the barn. She was tugging on the iron handle with all her might, but the door wouldn't budge.

This is it, I thought. *This is our chance to practice.*

"We should help her open the door," I commented to Damien. His hands were stuffed into the pockets of his black suit, so I placed my hand on the small of his back. *Damien's power can open the door.*

Mark was talking, saying something about apartments and turning old buildings into hubs for both living and working. I barely caught any of it because I was too busy conjuring. I watched as Laura tugged on the door handle again, and the barn door popped open so quickly she stumbled backward. She looked surprised for a moment, then she walked inside the barn and disappeared from view.

We did it! I wanted to high-five Damien.

Damien had a self-satisfied look on his face, and he was feeling good enough to be downright nice to Mark. "I'll be happy to mention your name to Emmett Kline. He'll find you a great place to live, I'm sure."

It was hard to continue the conversation when I wanted to do a happy dance instead, but I forced myself to say to Mark, "Surely whatever you're making as Trent's manager isn't a full-time income."

"No, but I've got some deals coming together."

"What kind of deals? You're not going to ditch the first client who helped you get back on your feet, are you?"

Mark looked incredulous. "Are you kidding? I'm counting on him being a part of them! This is for both of us. We're talking endorsements, official spokesperson opportunities…"

"How exciting for Trent," Damien said.

He wasn't wrong, but I also wondered how much the deals were really for Trent. Mark was awfully good at looking out for himself. Hopefully, things would work out for the best, for both of them.

"You should tell Trent what you have going on," I suggested. "That way, he's in the loop. Maybe he can think of some potential endorsements, too."

Mark nodded. "Smart. Yeah, I'll have a chat with him."

After that, I knew we could give Trent a fairly optimistic report, so Damien and I politely extracted ourselves from the conversation. We chattered happily all the way back to Cowboy's Corral. We had tested Damien's theory that I could help him control and guide his magic, and it had worked.

"Today, a barn door. Tomorrow, the world!" I said as I climbed out of his Corvette at the foot of the staircase to my apartment.

"I don't want to take over the world," Damien assured me with a wicked look. "Just Nightmare."

I walked up the stairs, feeling incredibly light and happy. I had helped Damien, and, more than that, I was getting to see him excited and optimistic. It was such a difference from the jerk he'd been when I had met him just a few months before.

"It worked," I said to my empty apartment when I went inside. "Our combined powers can really do things, and knowing that puts us that much closer to finding Baxter."

I had a bit of marketing work to do, and I wasted no time collecting my laptop and going to the office. Mama was as excited as I was when I told her about the barn door success, and it was hard for both of us to settle down and concentrate on our work after that.

I had finally focused my attention on my marketing tasks when my cell phone rang. I picked it up, expecting to see Damien's name, but instead, it was Zach's.

When I answered, he said tersely, "You need to get here, right now."

"To the Sanctuary?"

I could almost hear Zach's eyes rolling. "Obviously."

"I'll be right there! Is everything—" I didn't bother to finish asking my question because Zach had hung up.

"I have to go," I told Mama. I promised to let her know what was going on, because I didn't want her to worry.

I rushed back to my apartment, where I traded the laptop for my car keys. By the time I slid behind the wheel of my car, my chest was heaving. "I am too old for this kind of drama," I muttered as I started the car and threw it in reverse.

I took a cue from Damien's driving and pulled up right in front of the Sanctuary rather than heading for the staff parking area. Malcolm was standing in the shade under the portico, clearly on the lookout for me.

"What's wrong?" I asked breathlessly as I raced up to him.

"Nothing." Despite that reassurance, Malcolm walked so fast toward the dining room that his long black coat billowed out behind him. I had to jog to keep up, so by the time I made it into the dining room, I was breathing even harder.

I stopped short when I saw Damien and Zach standing close together at one of the tables, their backs to me. Both of their heads were bent, and I could tell they were talking to someone seated on the bench in front of them. I moved so I could see who it was, and I was shocked to find Laura sitting there. Long strands of hair had broken loose from her bun, like she had been tugging on it nervously.

Zach turned to me. "Olivia, Laura has something to say."

Laura looked up, and I saw a tear run down her cheek. "I'm the one who attacked Billy. But I'm not the one who killed him."

CHAPTER TWENTY-FIVE

It was a team effort! I was right! That thought was swiftly followed by a question. *But, if Laura was involved, then why is she confessing to us?* I didn't know the answer, of course, so I asked her.

Laura wiped at her face, leaving a streak of dirt where the tear had just been. She must have gotten the horses squared away after the two o'clock stunt show, then rushed straight to the Sanctuary without cleaning herself up first. "Zach and I were hanging out this morning, and he told me about the supernatural community here. I realized all of you would know what had made those claw marks on Billy."

"Laura has admitted to being the werewolf we saw on the dirt road," Malcolm told me.

"Zach kept sniffing me," Laura said. "At first, I thought he was just being weird, until I realized he and I were the same kind. And, if that were the case, then surely he and all the supernaturals in Nightmare would never accept the idea Billy had been attacked by a coyote." Laura lifted a hand and looked at her fingernails. "They can't cut the same way we can."

I sat down onto the bench a short distance from Laura. I should have been afraid of her. After all, she had just confessed to being a werewolf and the one who had left the deep gouges in Billy's body. For some reason, though, I felt curious rather than terrified. "Why did you attack Billy?"

"He was horrible to work with, right from the start." Laura sniffed and wiped at her nose as another tear escaped her eye. "Billy was on me constantly, saying I was grooming the horses the wrong way and not training them properly. He actually accused me of mistreating them. Can you believe that? Horses are my life. They're animals, yes, but they understand me, and I understand them. I would never treat them badly."

"You've alluded to Billy's behavior before," I noted. "He treated you the same way he treated Leo, right up until Billy convinced Norman to fire him. Why do you think he had such a problem with the show's trainers?"

"Honestly? I think Billy was having trouble performing some of the stunts. He had old injuries that made it difficult for him sometimes. Leo says Billy didn't used to throw around accusations like that, and he might have started doing it so he could blame anyone but himself when he blew a stunt."

"He'd rather get someone fired than admit to his own shortcomings," Damien grumbled. "What an egotistical jerk."

Laura nodded. "My thoughts exactly."

"Laura," Zach said gently, putting a hand on her shoulder, "you haven't told us yet why you attacked Billy that night."

"I was getting to that." Laura took a deep breath and squared her shoulders. "We all had to pull a lot of hours once Trent joined the show. Norman wanted the updates to roll out immediately, so it was a wild week of getting ready. I was working late one night in the barn when I heard Billy out in the corral, shouting. I thought he might disturb the horses, so I went out to see what he was hollering about."

"What was it?" I asked, leaning toward her with anticipation.

"Nothing. He was drunk and acting like an idiot. He claimed he was better than the new guy, and he said he was going to prove it. When he saw me, he demanded I saddle up Thorn, his favorite horse. I refused, of course, so he pushed past me into the barn and tried to do it himself."

Laura stopped and took another deep breath. When she spoke again, her voice wavered. "You have to understand! I was afraid he was going to hurt Thorn! He was so drunk and reckless. I tried to pull Billy away from Thorn, but he fought back. I got so upset that I transformed. It was that bad."

"Billy must have panicked when you turned into a werewolf right in front of him," I said.

Laura let out a sardonic laugh. "I turned while his back was to me, and he was so drunk he thought a wolf had snuck into the barn! That stupid man attacked me, and I fought him off as gently as I could. Finally, he gave up and ran off. I swear, I didn't kill him. I made some deep cuts with my claws, but nothing fatal."

"What did you do after he ran off?" Zach looked placid, as if he heard about werewolf attacks on a regular basis.

Actually, it was entirely possible he did.

"I stayed with the horses," Laura said. "I didn't want to leave them until I was sure Billy wasn't coming back. After nearly an hour, I figured it was safe, and I left."

Zach began to rub Laura's back slowly. I was inclined to believe her, and he obviously was, too. If he had been an animated character, his eyes would have been shaped like little hearts.

"If Billy had the claw marks before he was murdered," I mused, "then his killer must have purposely chosen a method that, at a glance, would still look like an animal attack."

Malcolm brought the tips of his pointer fingers together. "They used something long and thin, according to that newspaper article. The wounds probably blended right in with Laura's work."

"So we're still looking for a killer, but probably not one with claws." I looked around at my friends. "I guess that's progress."

"Indeed." Malcolm pushed a bony elbow against Zach's side. "Zach, why don't you show Laura where the ladies' room is? I'm sure she'd love to freshen up."

"Yeah, that would be great," Laura said, rising smoothly from the bench. "I'm sure I have mascara all over my cheeks."

"No, just dirt," Zach said reassuringly.

"I'm filling in for Zach as the Sanctuary's security guard this afternoon," Malcolm said, "so I've got to get to work." He gave me a little bow, then followed Zach and Laura out of the dining room.

Damien sat down next to me, taking the spot Laura had just vacated. "How strange that Trent and Laura both showed up here. If we wait long enough, everyone involved with the show will drop by and tell us unexpected news."

"It's not strange at all," I said. "The Sanctuary is a safe haven. Even people who don't live and work here can probably sense it. We take care of each other, we accept each other. That feeling—that vibe, as Mama would say—is probably something Trent and Laura picked up on subconsciously. They felt safe coming to us."

Damien suddenly looked sad. "Every single person here made me feel like part of the family, even when my father was teaching me to be as unlike them as possible. They accepted that he wanted me to bury my supernatural abilities and live like a normal person. And, instead of feeling grateful to everyone, I resented them and ran away from Nightmare as soon as I graduated high school." Damien blew out a slow breath as he looked toward the tall windows that offered a view of the wild area behind the Sanctuary. "Even when I came back, I acted like this place was a burden."

"You were a confused teenager with power you didn't understand," I said gently. "Your dad certainly didn't help the situation by teaching you to suppress your power without telling you what you were capable of or why he was afraid of it."

"It doesn't excuse my behavior."

I laid a hand on Damien's arm. "You also gave up your job and lost your relationship, all so you could come back to run a place you didn't want anything to do with. You acted like it was a burden because it was."

Damien gazed at me. "You left behind a husband and came here. I left behind a fiancée."

Despite the solemn subject, I couldn't stop the laugh that erupted from my mouth. "Let's hope she doesn't show up here, too! We've got so many exes running around Nightmare they could just about start their own bowling team."

Damien laughed, too, and I felt the tension in the room ease. "It's not quite that bad."

I saw a flash of movement to my left, and I looked over just in time to see a small book soaring through the air. Judging by its flight path, it had been sitting on the podium at the front of the room. I turned to Damien with one eyebrow raised. "Not that bad, huh?"

"All the talk about exes got me a little riled up."

"Then let's not talk about them anymore!" I slapped my hands on my thighs to drive home my point, then got up and searched for the book. It had skittered under one of the tables, and I had to practically do gymnastics to retrieve it. "Huh. This one landed open, too, just like those two books in your office."

"Does it also have a bookmark?" Damien asked.

"Yeah, but it's just a scrap of paper." I picked it up and waved it in the air. "Definitely not a clue to your dad's whereabouts."

"Maybe the bookmarks weren't the clues but the pages they're marking." Damien took the book out of my hands and looked at the cover. "Though I don't know what a bird-watching guide has to do with anything. Madge probably left this here. If she's never told you about bird omens before, you should ask her. It's a fascinating subject."

"Let's take another look at those first two books," I suggested. "Maybe we'll see if they all fit together somehow."

"Madge would tell you it's an omen from a"—Damien put a finger on the left-hand page—"golden pheasant."

"Come on." I led the way to Damien's office, and we soon had all three books lined up on his desk.

"So we have the bird guide, which had a bookmark between the pages for pheasants and a bird called a Phoebe." I pointed at the latest book Damien had turned into a literal paper airplane.

"And this one," Damien said, fingering the spine of the dark-green book, "is about supernatural creatures. Considering the pages that had the envelope shoved between them contain entries from *Oread* to *Qilin*, there are a lot of possible clues."

"And then we have this book of antique maps." I opened it to where the note from the tailor was. "This is a map of Phoenix from 1869. Your dad was in the Arizona Territory by then, so maybe he lived there for a while. Oh! Maybe we need to go there…to look for a bird…that is actually a legendary creature. Oh, that's stupid. None of it makes sense!"

"It's not the map that matters," Damien said. He was taking quick, shallow breaths. "Do you remember the first time you heard my father's voice?"

"Of course. I heard it when I was passing by the mine."

"And what did that voice say?"

"'My ashes are my own.' You and Malcolm have said it was sort of a catch-phrase for Baxter, whenever he felt like he was being challenged."

"Your guess was right. There is a legendary creature that looks like a bird, and it can burn to nothing but ash." Damien picked up the map book and held it toward me. "My father is a phoenix."

CHAPTER TWENTY-SIX

"A phoenix?" I repeated. "Like you just said, they're birds. Baxter sure looks human in every photo I've seen of him."

"They are birds. I didn't even know they existed, let alone that they could take human form." Damien dropped the map book and picked up the one about legendary creatures. "It's right here on this marked page. Why did my father mark pages in books to lead us to what he is? He was always so secretive about his supernatural origins."

"Maybe he knew this day would come."

"That he would disappear?"

"If Baxter knew he was in danger, then maybe he left clues so we could find him if anything ever happened to him. Somehow, him being a phoenix is a clue to tracking him down."

Damien poked a finger against his chest. "I'm half bird."

"And half psychic," I reminded him. Then, I gasped. "Of course! Your mother has been manipulating your outbursts of psychic power, like you suggested! She knew Baxter left these clues, and she's been trying to show them to us."

"She's guiding us. Why didn't she show up six months ago to help, when my father first went missing?"

"Because you weren't here," I said. Somehow, I knew

that was the right answer. "And once you were here, you weren't ready yet. Even giving us the clues like this is allowing us to explore your power. Otherwise, she could have simply communicated through Tanner and McCrory, like she's done before. She's helping you, but she's also making sure you continue to practice your abilities."

"We need to talk to someone who might know how this information helps us," Damien said. "And I think the right person is the one who knew my father the best."

"Malcolm," I said, nodding.

I had expected Damien to go off in search of him, but instead, he pushed one of the brass buttons on the wall behind him. The hospital's old call system had been set up for the residents of the Sanctuary, and I didn't need to see the yellowing, hand-written label next to the button Damien had his finger on. I'd only ever seen him use the system to call Tanner and McCrory.

The two ghosts materialized just a few seconds later. McCrory tipped his hat. "Sir, ma'am. What can we do for you?"

"Hey, Miss Olivia," Tanner cut in, "is it true your former husband is here in Nightmare? Rumor has it he visited the Sanctuary the other night, but I must have missed him."

I sighed. Even the ghosts knew the gossip about Mark. Were there no secrets in Nightmare?

Damien ignored Tanner and said, "I need Malcolm here, now. Please"—the ghosts sailed through the wall where the fireplace was, and Damien looked at the spot as he finished his sentence—"go find him."

"Those two have been around here for a long time, right?" I asked. "Malcolm and Baxter were already living in Nightmare when the ghosts had their shootout on High Noon Boulevard. They might know something, too."

Damien shook his head. "My father discovered the box

with their six-shooters in an antique store, back in the nineteen seventies or eighties, I think. The ghosts haven't been living here at the Sanctuary for all that long."

By the time Malcolm rushed into the room, Damien and I had both started pacing. Damien was doing it behind his desk, while I had taken up a route between the fireplace and the opposite wall.

"The ghosts said it's an emergency," Malcolm stated as he came to a stop.

When Damien looked at Malcolm, there was a smile tugging at the corners of his mouth. "Not an emergency. A breakthrough. My father is a phoenix."

Malcolm's mouth fell open. His eyes were fixed on Damien, but they had a faraway look. He was probably seeing memories of Baxter in his mind. "It makes so much sense," he finally said. "How did I not see it myself? Being a phoenix is what allowed him to do this."

"Do what?" I asked.

Malcolm spread both hands. "This. The Sanctuary. I always knew Baxter must be incredibly powerful, because it would take a lot of magic and a lot of willpower to bring all these supernatural creatures together. Not every supernatural community is as good as ours. As harmonious."

"My father used his power to create a safe haven." Damien looked at me significantly, and I knew he was thinking about our conversation earlier, when I had used those exact words to describe the Sanctuary.

"Phoenixes are remarkably rare," Malcolm continued. "I'm rare, for that matter, but I'd be willing to bet there are more wendigos in the world than there are phoenixes. They're valuable, too. Their feathers, their ashes, their tears…"

"Ashes!" I was practically shouting in my excitement. "That phrase of Baxter's, 'my ashes are my own,' it must be in reference to his vulnerability. He knew he would be a target because his ashes have value."

"And that's probably why he's missing now," Damien finished for me. "Someone out there wants what he has. If it's his ashes, though, then wouldn't he have to…" Damien trailed off, but he brought both hands up, his fingers spread wide.

"Burn, yes," Malcolm said, nodding. "Don't worry, though. That wouldn't kill him, since he would be reborn from the ashes. The question is, if he was taken so those ashes could be sold on the black market, are they making him go through death and rebirth over and over again?"

I shuddered. "How awful. Also, black market? Seriously?"

"Oh, yes," Malcolm said. "There's a robust supernatural black market in North America. Collectors sell things from curses to, well, phoenix ashes."

"That's disturbing, but this helps us," I said. "Now we have a better idea where to search."

Malcolm gave us both a little salute. "Now, if you'll excuse me, it's nearly time for the family meeting. Olivia, are you working tonight? I'd be happy to escort you to the dining room."

"Thanks, but I'm off tonight. You have fun scaring people!"

"I will! And, as soon as we close tonight, I'll begin doing research in the library to see if we can learn anything else about phoenixes that will help us."

Malcolm glided out the door as I rounded on Damien. "This place has a library?"

"Filled with books about every supernatural topic you could ever want to learn about. I'll show you later."

"In the meantime, you still have that present from Mark." I nodded toward the box, which Damien had swept onto the floor to make room for the three books. "Want to get in some quick practice?"

Damien lifted the box gingerly and dropped it in the middle of his desk.

"It's not going to hurt you," I said.

"Maybe not physically. What did you ever see in him, anyway?"

"Like I keep telling myself, he didn't used to be like this. It's like his worst, schmoozy salesman qualities have been exaggerated."

"Before I rip this box open and my emotions skyrocket, what do we want to practice?"

"Umm." I looked around the room. "Ooh, I know! Let's see if we can channel your power into sliding that photo on the mantel from one end to the other. You've moved that photo before, and it will take control from both of us to keep it from falling to the floor."

Damien was shaking his head before I had finished. "There's glass in that frame. I'm not risking it. Let's move the rock, instead."

What Damien called a rock was actually a small chunk of unrefined copper. It was attached to a wood base that had a brass plate on it. I squinted at the text on the plate, then took a step back. "I need reading glasses," I mumbled. "But it looks like this copper came from Sonny's Folly Mine. How about that? It's from your house!"

"And it won't shatter if it falls off the mantel." Damien took the gold bow off the box. "Let's get this over with."

I moved close to Damien, ready to grab his hand and conjure his control the moment he saw Mark's present.

Damien ripped off the green paper and opened the box.

I tensed, ready for objects in the room around me to start vibrating.

Instead, Damien threw back his head and laughed.

CHAPTER TWENTY-SEVEN

Damien was still laughing as he reached into the box and pulled out a Western shirt like the ones Mark and Trent had been wearing lately. This one was made from an orange and black plaid, and it had acid-green fringe dangling from the sleeves.

I was too horrified to laugh. It was the ugliest piece of clothing I had ever seen in my life.

Damien turned the shirt toward me, and I saw a stylized haunted house embroidered in the same acid-green color on each of the black lapels. "Halloween colors," Damien said, gasping for breath. "For our haunted house."

"It's scarier than anything we have here," I commented. "Oh, I bet you anything Mark has some Western wear deal in the works. He was probably pitching a clothing company the day Trent overheard Mark talking about using him as leverage. Trent would be the spokesperson for a line of the tackiest shirts ever made."

"And if I've learned anything about Mark, he wants to make a bit of commission by outfitting everyone at the Sanctuary in matching shirts." Damien waved the shirt dramatically. "This is just the first of many!"

I made a gagging noise. "I'll stick with the usual Sanctuary T-shirt, thank you very much."

"Am I supposed to send him a thank-you note, or

what?" Damien asked as he dropped the shirt back into the box.

"If the deal goes through, I'm sure Trent's ex-wife will be sending Mark a thank-you note. She'll get her payday right after Trent does."

"She probably knew Trent would have a lot more endorsement opportunities if he was the star of the show," Damien pointed out.

"And all she had to do was get Billy out of the way. Don't worry, she's still on my suspect list, but this clothing deal is just speculation. Until we know for sure what Mark has up his sleeve, there's no point in me going to have another chat with Stacy."

I heard a loud, rapid *tick-tick-tick* sound from the hallway, and a second later, Felipe bounded into the room. He jumped up onto one of the chairs and pressed his snout against my hip. I figured that was his way of asking for me to pet him, so I complied.

Mori entered the room with less noise and less haste. I could only hear the rustle of her burgundy silk gown, which made her look like a princess from a fairy tale. A dark fairy tale, where the heroine had fangs and drank blood, but a fairytale, nonetheless.

"Malcolm said you were in here," Mori said to me. "You have a visitor."

Mori's tone was so flat I didn't need to ask who it was. "Speak of the devil," I muttered.

"Not the kind of practice session I wanted to have," Damien commented.

"I can tell him you're out sick, or on a date, or—oh, good heavens, Damien, what is that awful thing in the box?" Mori had stepped up to Damien's desk, and she was staring into the box with a look of absolute disgust.

"It's a shirt. From Mark." Damien looked like he was torn between amusement and dismay.

Mori lifted the shirt, her full red lips turning down farther the longer she gazed at it. "I didn't think I'd ever see one of these again."

"You've seen shirts like this before?" I asked.

"Of course. They used to be all over this town, but that was years ago. One day, they were gone. It was like they disappeared overnight."

"Probably because no one was buying them," Damien said.

"Or because the owner ran out of money," I added. I reached out and took the shirt from Mori. Sure enough, there was a *Wilder West* logo on the inside of the collar. "Billy had wanted to start his own line of Western wear. I'm guessing he launched the line locally but never got farther than that."

"Maybe he was killed for having bad taste," Mori said. Felipe growled, as if in agreement.

"Billy was embezzling from the show, and we know he somehow lost his family fortune," I continued. "He probably dumped all that money into the clothing line, only for it to fail, anyway."

Mori put the shirt down and pointed toward Damien. "He had one of the shirts."

"What?" Damien and I said in unison.

"Oh, yeah. Damien, you were probably too small to remember, but your dad bought you one of these, along with the cutest little cowboy hat. Olivia, I know you think the company lost money because no one was buying, but I assure you, these shirts were all the rage for about a year. I lost count of the number of tourists I fed off who were wearing one of these."

"Ew." I knew Mori mesmerized tourists so she could drink their blood, but I didn't like hearing about it. At least, I reminded myself, she only took a little, so the tourists lived happily ever after, with no memory of the encounter and only two tiny puncture wounds on their neck.

"Then it seems," Damien said, "the clothing line is being revived, and Mark is obviously a part of it. We were just saying Trent's ex-wife might have paved the way for this to happen."

"And by paved the way," Mori said with a smirk, "you mean she killed the man who was standing in the way of Trent's rising star."

"And the rising balance in his bank account." I nodded. "But then, we also have to consider everyone else involved with the show. If this clothing line can be successful again, it can only be a benefit for everyone working there. The show's popularity will grow along with the popularity of the clothing."

"Who are we going to confront first?" Mori asked with a wicked smile.

"Mark," I said.

Mori gasped. "You think he did it? To put his client front and center?"

"No. I mean, I hear him in the hallway, so he's found us." I didn't know how I recognized the sound of Mark's footsteps. Years of marriage to him, I supposed.

Sure enough, Mark strutted into the room at that moment. He had on a blue windbreaker, and a long blue-and-white scarf hung around his neck. "I had no idea it got so cold in the desert! I should have brought more of my jackets with me. Oh, Damien. I see you got the shirt. Isn't it great?"

Justine was right behind Mark, and I lifted the shirt briefly to show it to her. Justine's cheeks puffed out as she fought to hold in a laugh.

The photo on the mantel and the chunk of copper began to vibrate, and I moved around Damien's desk and took his hand. *We have got to work on me conjuring for him without needing to maintain physical contact.*

Even as I was thinking that, Mark said, "Do you have to do that in front of me?"

Mark thinks Damien and I are dating.

My instinct was to drop Damien's hand, but he only tightened his fingers around mine. "Olivia didn't ask you to come to this town, and she certainly didn't ask you to be a part of her new life here. She has the right to do whatever she wants."

I squeezed Damien's hand in gratitude. "My home is here now, Mark. These people are my family. Why would I want to hide that from anyone?"

Mark muttered something about family and being in the middle of nowhere as his face clouded over. "I thought I'd get a better welcome from you, Olivia. I thought you'd understand."

I felt bad about hurting Mark's feelings, but Damien was right. I had started a new life in a new town. Mark was the one who had decided to insert himself right into the middle of it. "I'm sorry, Mark," I said sincerely. "I'm not trying to hurt you. I'm trying to live my life. This is my job, and these are my friends."

Justine and Mori were both looking at me proudly. When I caught Justine's eye, she mouthed, "You go, girl!"

"Fine. Then I'll leave you alone." Mark flipped his scarf over his shoulder, nearly hitting Mori in the face with it. As Mori glared at him, I stared at Mark.

"Oh, no. How could I have been so blind?" I cried.

Mark paused and looked at me hopefully, like I was about to open my arms to him and tell him he should stick around Nightmare forever. Instead, what I said was, "I know how Billy died! And if I'm right, then I know who did it, too!"

CHAPTER TWENTY-EIGHT

Mark looked utterly confused, but Justine was already turning toward the door. I dropped Damien's hand and ran past Mark. I caught up to Justine halfway down the hallway, and she said, "Who's driving?"

"We'll need two cars if we're all going!"

Justine's pace slowed. "Where are we going, anyway? Who did it?"

"We're going to—" I skidded to a stop as we came to the end of the hallway. Trent and Darla were just walking through the door.

Clara, who was getting ready to take tickets when the Sanctuary opened in just a few minutes, called to me. "They say they're here to see Damien."

I heard Damien's voice behind me. "They are?"

I groaned. "Mark, did you all come here to give a sales pitch?"

"You saw that shirt!" Mark said. He had followed us down the hall, and he quickly plastered his salesman expression onto his face. "This is an opportunity to brand Nightmare Sanctuary as the preeminent Western haunted house."

"I don't care about the shirts, Mark," I said firmly. "It's your scarf that caught my eye."

Mark touched a hand to his scarf, his smile faltering. "You want to have staff scarves?" Then, his face brightened as he considered it. "Sure, why not? You could have thick ones for the wintertime, and lighter, summer scarves during the hot months."

"What I really want to know," I said, "is whether Darla knit the scarf you're wearing with the same needles she used to kill Billy."

Mark stared at me blankly. Darla, on the other hand, stepped toward me. "How dare you?"

"You offered to repair Stacy's damaged sweater," I said to Darla. "She even commented that she wanted to learn how to knit. Just now, Mark shifted his scarf, and I saw the tag stitched on it. It's the same logo that's on all these Western shirts. Wilder West, the clothing line Billy tried to launch so many years ago."

"What does the logo have to do with anything?" Darla spat.

"It's not just about the logo, Darla. It's also about the fact that Billy wasn't killed by an animal. He was stabbed with something long and thin." I reached toward Mark and lifted one end of his scarf. "Something like knitting needles. You didn't just make some designs for him, did you? You had a stake in the company, which is why you're still using the logo."

Darla sputtered, her face growing red. She was a small woman, but in that moment, she looked dangerous, like a feral cat that had been cornered. "You're making a lot of assumptions."

"I am," I admitted. "But they're assumptions that make sense. You needed Billy out of the way. His star was falling, as you told me yourself. He was getting too old and beat up for the job, and you knew he couldn't be the face of the brand if you tried to relaunch it. But if you had someone young and charming, someone who was on his way up, then he could take you and your shirts on the ride to fame and fortune. How long did you wait before you proposed a partnership to Mark and Trent? Was Billy's body even cold?"

"He ruined my dreams!" Darla screeched. Her hands were curled into fists, and Trent wisely stepped sideways so he was out of arm's reach. "He kept investing more money into the business, and he said it was no problem. But he wasted his fortune on dumb things we didn't need. Then, to make it worse, he started embezzling from the show to fund the business. He ruined everything."

"Did you know about the embezzling?" Damien asked Darla.

She shook her head. "Not until Norman found out and blackmailed Billy into coming back to Nightmare. During the time Billy was working at the theme park in California, our sales kept going up and up. The show out there had bigger audiences, and the park let us sell the shirts at their shop. When Billy left to come back here, the theme park canceled our deal. We were back to being small-town nobodies, and we had no money left to make another go of it. I've been saving for years to try again."

"But you had to get Billy out of the way first," I said.

"He owned the trademark. When I offered to buy it from him, he refused. He said that if I tried to launch the line without him, he'd sue me. I did what I had to do."

Trent's face had been getting more and more pale, and he grabbed Clara's arm to steady himself. "You killed Billy so I could help you rebuild your clothing business?" There was no trace of Trent's usual confidence and charisma.

"I could have started a brand-new company, but I wanted that original Wilder West name and logo. People would remember it from back then, and their nostalgia would make them want to buy. I hadn't planned to kill Billy, but I was working late that night, and he barged into my costuming room, drunk as a skunk. He was bleeding, bad. He said he'd been attacked by a wolf."

"And you saw your opportunity," Mori said. She, Justine, and Clara were standing together in a clump, watching the scene with horror and fascination. Trent was still clinging to Clara.

Darla looked in Mori's direction. "I tried to help him. I sat him down and gave him some water, thinking he might sober up. He ranted and raved for about an hour, and then he laid into me about the clothing line. That was the last straw, and I knew if I was careful, the police would see claw marks, not stab wounds. I grabbed my strongest knitting needle and told Billy to lead me to where the attack had happened. I couldn't kill him right there in the costume department, obviously. Once we were inside the corral"—Darla shrugged—"he was too drunk to put up much of a fight."

According to Darla's timeline, Laura had just missed being witness to a murder. By the time Darla acted, Laura had just gone home, convinced Billy was gone and no longer a threat to the horses.

Darla had been smart, but she hadn't counted on the police doing an autopsy. Otherwise, Billy's death would have been chalked up to an animal attack, and she would have literally gotten away with murder.

Mark gave a cry of distress, and his knees buckled. Damien grabbed him under the arms just in time to keep him from falling to the ground.

"Guy can't even handle one little murder," Mori commented.

Darla looked like she was considering making a run for it, but Mori took one step toward her, and she seemed to shrink by a few inches. Trent and Damien—who had propped Mark against the wall—joined Mori, forming a loose circle around Darla, and Justine called the police.

"We were supposed to open five minutes ago," Clara pointed out as we waited for the Nightmare Police Department to arrive.

"I don't think we'll get any complaints," Damien said, his eyes never leaving Darla. "The people in line are definitely getting their money's worth tonight."

I was both disappointed and relieved that Officer Reyes wasn't one of the police officers who showed up to arrest Darla. He would have made some comment about me still being involved in this murder case, but at the same time, I knew he would have given me a pat on the back. Still, it felt good to see Darla escorted out the front door in handcuffs. I didn't need praise from Reyes to feel a deep sense of satisfaction.

As soon as Darla and the police were gone, Clara began to let guests through the door. The crowd was buzzing with everything they had just witnessed as Justine and Mori scurried away to take up their posts inside the haunt.

Trent and Mark both had shocked expressions on their faces. "You've been through this before?" Mark asked. "Catching a murderer?"

"A few times," I said.

"But... Darla?" Trent's voice cracked as he said her name. "She seemed so nice."

"She did," I agreed. "She was also eager to have a life beyond taking in shirts and trousers for stunt riders, and Billy was in her way."

"We'll go tell Norman in person," Mark said. Right then, he looked and sounded like the old Mark I had known. Smart, responsible, and not trying to hide behind a bright and shiny facade. He nodded at Damien and me. "We'll talk soon."

By the time Mark and Trent had disappeared out the front door, the queue inside the entryway was half full. I kept hearing the words *police* and *arrest* from people winding back and forth between the velvet ropes.

"I'm going to build a bonfire out back," Damien said. When I gave him a quizzical look, he added, "I want to burn that horrible shirt."

I chuckled. "I'm glad you can turn your focus to the important things, now that we've caught the killer."

"The bonfire isn't just for that. The rest of the staff will know the news soon enough, and it will give us a chance to unwind and discuss everything after we close for the night."

"By everything, do you mean just Darla's confession, or the news that your dad is a phoenix, too?"

"Everything," Damien said firmly. "There's a lot of supernatural knowledge between everyone here, and the more people we have helping us, the sooner we're going to find him."

"First, though, I never did tell you my news." I stepped close to Damien and curled a hand around his arm. I thought about leading him away so we could talk in private, but I didn't want to wait any longer. Instead, I kept my voice low enough that we wouldn't be overheard. "Your mother spoke to me yesterday."

Damien's lips parted, but he didn't say anything. I told him the words I had heard like a whisper in my ear, seemingly in answer to my thoughts about what Damien and I might be capable of doing together.

When I was finished, Damien pulled me into a tight hug. Soon, he was the one whispering in my ear, rather than Lucille. "Thank you." His voice was tight with emotion, and I gave him a reassuring squeeze.

"I should have told you sooner, but there's been so much going on," I said when Damien finally released me. "You go start the bonfire. Since I'm not working tonight, I'll start putting together snacks and drinks to take out there. Even though we have a lot of work ahead of us, we still have a lot to celebrate."

CHAPTER TWENTY-NINE

"He's really gone?" Mori asked. She had just walked into the dining room, Felipe bounding along at her heels. It had already been two days since Darla's arrest, and I was happily settled at a table with Malcolm and Gunnar as we waited for that night's family meeting to begin.

"He really is," I said with satisfaction. "Mark is on his way back to Nashville."

"What a wild ride this has been," Gunnar commented.

"Even wilder than the ride I got from you!" I laughed. "Though I might ask you to take me flying again. That was scary but amazing."

A smile lit up Gunnar's stony face. "I'd be happy to."

"You must be relieved," Mori continued.

"I am. At the same time, I'm strangely grateful for Mark showing up here. It proved that I am absolutely, completely over him and my old life in Nashville. Plus, if it wasn't for Mark, we wouldn't know that I can help Damien control his power. And if Damien hadn't gotten upset about Mark, we might still be waiting for those books to come off the shelves."

"We know what Baxter is thanks to your ex-husband," Malcolm said thoughtfully. "It's strange, but somehow appropriate. You got some closure by seeing Mark again, but at the same time, he helped you open the next chapter."

"Literally, with the flying books," I quipped.

"I didn't like him," Mori said frankly. "You can do better."

Damien came into the room on the heels of that statement, and Mori raised her eyebrows at me. "As I said."

"A much better choice," Malcolm agreed, eyeing Damien with approval.

Damien stepped up to the table and looked from Mori to Malcolm. "What?"

"We were just saying that we like you better than Mark," Malcolm said.

If I had Damien's psychic powers, every bench in the room would have fallen over from the strength of my embarrassment.

"That's a surprise," Damien answered, seemingly unruffled by the implication. "The last I heard, you all thought I was a jerk.

Mori winked at Damien. "You're growing on us."

"Plus," Malcolm pointed out, "you've been much less of a jerk lately."

Damien gestured toward me. "I think that's Olivia's influence. She keeps me calm."

"And less jerky!" I added. Impulsively, I reached out and squeezed Damien's hand. My hand had been in his so often the past week that it didn't feel awkward anymore. Instead, it felt comforting. I had been relieved to realize the witches' dream about me and love had been about Mark's arrival in Nightmare. When they had warned me to be careful with my heart, they hadn't meant Damien, at all.

"I was waiting for both of you to be here to share some news," Gunnar said, looking at Damien and me. "I used to know a guy who had connections to the supernatural black market. His teeth were required for certain revenge spells, and he'd regularly sell them to dealers for cash. The teeth always grew back, so it was no big deal for him."

"Lucky guy." It was Theo, who had, as usual, snuck up without any of us noticing. He opened his mouth and ran his tongue along his filed-down fangs. Unfortunately for him, vampires didn't regenerate their teeth. The vampire hunter who had destroyed his fangs had probably known that.

"Anyway," Gunnar continued, "I'm going to reach out to the guy to see if he can help us. Maybe he's heard of a dealer with a sudden influx of phoenix ashes, feathers, or something else that will point us in the right direction."

Justine swept up at that moment, a notebook in her hands and a slightly harried expression on her face. "The meeting is starting in a few minutes, but how about we all catch up after work at Under the Undertaker's? Zach is meeting Laura there, and she really wants to get to know all of us."

"Ooh!" we all chorused in a singsong tone. Zach had been teasing me about Damien for weeks, and I was looking forward to getting some revenge.

I looked at Damien questioningly. He almost never went out with us after work.

"Fine, I'll go," he said. He was trying to look grumpy about it, but I knew better. Maybe hearing Mori's praise had been good for him, and it would help him work past his feeling of always being an outsider at the Sanctuary. He was one of us, especially since he had stopped tamping down his supernatural abilities.

Felipe rested his head on my leg, and I sat back and watched my friends chatting with each other. A deep feeling of peace and belonging came over me, and I blinked hard a few times to clear the tears I felt forming. The chance to go back to Nashville had landed on my doorstep, quite literally. Mark had shown up at my apartment and asked me to go back with him.

"Come home, Olivia," he had begged.

"I am home," I had told him.

I was so absorbed in the memory that I must have said the words out loud, because Justine waved her notebook toward me. "Yeah, you are. And I hope you like lots of bangle bracelets, because Vivian is off tonight, and I've got you down to take her spot as the psychic in the cabin scene."

I grinned and waved my hands in the air. "I foresee great things in our future!"

A NOTE FROM THE AUTHOR

How are we six books into this series already? I had so much fun writing this one, and I'm excited that you are now "in the know" about what Baxter is! I've known since book one, and it's been hard keeping that secret!

Please consider leaving a review for *Clawing at the Corral*. Reviews help other paranormal cozy fans find their next read, and I am so grateful for every one.

Eternally Yours,

Beth

P.S. You can keep up with my latest book news, get fun freebies, and more by signing up for my newsletter at BethDolgner.com!

FIND OUT WHAT'S NEXT FOR OLIVIA AND THE RESIDENTS OF NIGHTMARE, ARIZONA!

Axing at the Antique Store

NIGHTMARE, ARIZONA BOOK SEVEN
PARANORMAL COZY MYSTERIES

Ghosts, gossip, and grim omens in Nightmare, Arizona.

It's never good when a banshee senses a death on the horizon. When that death coincides with the arrival of a frightening new supernatural creature in Nightmare, Arizona, everyone at Nightmare Sanctuary Haunted House is on high alert.

Olivia Kendrick and her friends just wanted to go shopping at the local antique store. Instead, they wind up embroiled in a murder investigation that hints at some sinister dealings in the old mining town. It seems like everyone had a reason to want the owner of the antique store dead.

While Olivia tracks down clues with the help of her growing conjuring skills, she also makes an important discovery about Damien Shackleford's supernatural abilities. Will Olivia's boss be able to use his powers to find his missing father, Baxter?

Before he can do that, though, Damien will have to keep Olivia safe when she becomes the target for a vengeful suspect…

ACKNOWLEDGMENTS

Wow, did my test readers catch some big huge plot holes this time around! Alex, Kristine, David, Lisa, Sabrina, and Mom: thanks for your eyeballs and enthusiasm. Lia at Your Best Book Editor and Trish at Blossoming Pages, I'm so grateful for your editing and suggestions. My ARC readers: thank you for all the release-week love! And, last but not least, thanks to Jena at BookMojo for the beautiful covers, graphics, and formatting.

ABOUT THE AUTHOR

Beth Dolgner writes paranormal fiction and nonfiction. Her interest in things that go bump in the night really took off on a trip to Savannah, Georgia, so it's fitting that her first series—Betty Boo, Ghost Hunter—takes place in that spooky city. Beth also writes paranormal nonfiction, including her first book, *Georgia Spirits and Specters*, which is a collection of Georgia ghost stories.

Beth and her husband, Ed, live in Tucson, Arizona. They're close enough to Tombstone that Beth can easily visit its Wild West street and watch staged shootouts, all in the name of research for the Nightmare, Arizona series.

Beth also enjoys giving presentations on Victorian death and mourning traditions as well as Victorian Spiritualism. She has been a volunteer at an historic cemetery, a ghost tour guide, and a paranormal investigator.

Keep up with Beth and sign up for her newsletter at BethDolgner.com.

BOOKS BY BETH DOLGNER

The Nightmare, Arizona Series

Paranormal Cozy Mystery

Homicide at the Haunted House

Drowning at the Diner

Slaying at the Saloon

Murder at the Motel

Poisoning at the Party

Clawing at the Corral

Axing at the Antique Store

The Eternal Rest Bed and Breakfast Series

Paranormal Cozy Mystery

Sweet Dreams

Late Checkout

Picture Perfect

Scenic Views

Breakfast Included

Groups Welcome

Quiet Nights

The Betty Boo, Ghost Hunter Series

Romantic Urban Fantasy

Ghost of a Threat

Ghost of a Whisper

Ghost of a Memory

Ghost of a Hope

Manifest

Young Adult Steampunk

A Talent for Death

Young Adult Urban Fantasy

Nonfiction

Georgia Spirits and Specters

Everyday Voodoo

Made in United States
Troutdale, OR
03/12/2025